WRITER AND ILLUSTRATOR
CARLA SPEED MCNEIL

REMOVER OF OBSTACLES
MICHAEL MCNEIL
GRAPHIC DESIGNER
VINCE SNEED

FINDER VOLUME 1: SIN-EATER

Most of the material reprinted within appeared originally in issues 1-7 of the magazine series **FINDER**, 1996-1999, © Carla Speed McNeil.

Book design by Vince Sneed.

Published by Lightspeed Press
P.O. Box 448
Annapolis Junction, MD 20701

Second printing, October 2001

Bound in Canada

ISBN 0-9673691-0-X

FINDER

SIN-EATER, VOLUME ONE

FOR MICHAEL, FOR EVERYTHING

SALUTATION

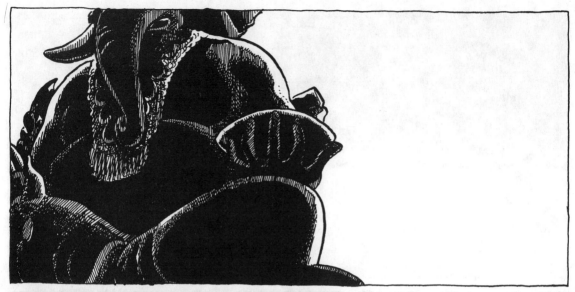

≈HAAAAHH⋯

AH≈A≈AOW!
SH:T!

≈PTCH!≈

WELL, SIR ⋯

I CAN'T MAKE YOU A PROPER OFFERING, 'CAUSE I DON'T KNOW WHAT YOUR PLEASURE IS.

I DUNNO YOUR NAME OR WHY YOU'RE OUT HERE--

--BUT YOU KEEP THE HEAT A LONG TIME AFTER THE SUN'S DOWN SO I'M GRATEFUL.

-AH!-

USUALLY WHILE I WAS LIVING IN
THE BADLANDS I WAS UP AND
ABOUT ONLY AFTER DARK.

4

THE HEAT OF THE DAY IS INCREDIBLE, AND YOU LOSE MORE WATER THAN YOU'LL EVER FIND. AT NIGHT, THOUGH, THE DESERT TAKES ON A WEIRD NEON BLUE GLOW AND EVERYTHING WAKES UP. **EVERYTHING.** BIGGER, NASTIER CREATURES THAN YOU'D THINK LIVE OUT HERE, AND MY OWN FOOLISHNESS GOT ME TOO CLOSE TO ONE.

STILL, I **DID** GET MIGHTY CLOSE TO HER, AND THOUGH SHE GOT ME PRETTY GOOD, SHE DIDN'T KILL ME, SO IT WAS WORTH IT.

BUT I WAS A MESS, AND I'D STAYED SIX MONTHS INSTEAD OF SIX WEEKS AS I'D PLANNED. FELT LIKE TIME TO DO SOMETHING ELSE.

I FOUND MYSELF CLOSE TO THE NORTHERN FOOTHILLS AND SOMETHING SAID "GO SEE EMMA" SO I WENT.

WARNING
NOTHING
NO SERVICES
NEXT 962 m

HUH!

WELL, THERE HE IS.

PAY UP.

WEIRD PLACE,
IS ANVARD.

LIKE ANY CITY.

YOU **ARE** ON THE CLOTH.

HA-HA...

THAT'S YOUR BEST OFFER? HELL, WHAT'S YOUR WORST?

HEY! HEY, KID, WHATCHA WANT FOR THAT RON CHITIN ROOKIE CARD?

"NOTHING WRONG WITH THIS CITY THAT A GOOD PLAGUE WOULDN'T FIX," SEZEE.

"I'LL BE BACK WHEN THE CITY COUNCIL STRIPS DOWN AN' DANCES THE HULLY-GULLY AROUND THE BLACK ANGEL MONUMENT", SEZEE.

WELL, EVVYBODDY, HEEE'S BACK. BIG AS LIFE AND TWICE AS NATURAL.

"SO, ALL BILL COLLECTORS, REPO AGENTS, FORMAL VENDETTAS AND ANGRY HUS-BANDS ARE DULY NOTIFIED. ANYTHING TO ADD, MR. JAEGER AYERS?"

AHH, BITE ME, RUTHIE. GO FIND YOURSELF SOME NICE CAR-WRECK VICTIMS TO INTERVIEW. OKAY, KID?

CHANNEL C22

"THESE ARE THE PEOPLE IN YOUR NEIGHBORHOOD."

THANKEW, THANKEW!

MOVING RIGHT ALONG, WE BRING YOU TO JOSIE "JO-JO" JIMBROWSKI, FORMER CHILD STAR TURNED WRAX PUSHER.

WE'RE ALL HAPPY TO HEAR OF YOUR NEW OUTPATIENT STATUS, MS. JIMBROWSKI!

TEN FOR ONE, FIFTEEN FOR BOTH.

ALL RIGHT, FEZHEAD. PRESENT YOUR LICENSE AS REQUIRED BY LAW.

MARIN WARDEN

NOT HARDLY. I'M A FREE TRADER.

WHORESHIT. YOU'RE ABOUT AS INDIAN AS PRUNE POP-TARTS, YA TRENDY-ASS WANNA-BE WHITE BOY.

"WANNA-BE WHITE BOY..."

OOH **BOY**! WE GOT OURSELVES A FINE, **FINE** EXAMPLE OF A CULTURE COP **HERE**! GONNA SPARE THESE NICE TOURISTS THE PAAIIN OF BUYIN' WHATEVER THEIR TRANSIENT LITTLE HEARTS DESIRE **AND** BE A NOBLE FRIEND TO THE DWELLERS IN THE WILDERNESS **TOO**?

O-KAY. YOU GOT IT, WISEASS—

WHO EVER TOLD YOU "HEY, **YOU** ARE THE ULTIMATE **GOD-BOSS** OF WHO **LOOKS** INDIAN ENOUGH TO BE ONE? DIDJA EVER STOP TO THINK IT **MIGHT** NOT BE **RIGHT** FOR PEOPLE TO HAVE TO DRAG OUT SACRED CEREMONIAL CLOTHING OR DYE THEIR SKIN WITH ALL KINDS OF TOXIC CRAP JUST TO LOOK "INDIAN" ENOUGH TO PLEASE ASS-HOLES LIKE **YOU** WHO DON'T EVEN KNOW WHAT THEY'RE LOOKING AT?

WHAT'S UP?

FIGHT

FISH

HA!

CRUNK

POP

FUMP

CLAP CLAP CLAP
WHOOOO

THAT'S FOR EVERY LITTLE OL' LADY WHO WASN'T WEARIN' ENOUGH TURQUOISE, YA GREASEBRAIN!

CLAP CLAP
CLAP
FEEEEE
CLAP CLAP
CLAP CLAP CLAP

GUM-BALL

CLAP CLAP
CLAP
HA-HA-HA HAHA~
CLAP CLAP CLAP
CLAP

I'LL JUST SPEND IT ON GIN & CIGARETTES

HA HA
HA~AWK
HAK HAK

I'LL JUST SPEND IT ON GIN & CIGARETTES

C'MON, GRANDAD. GUESS I COULD GO FOR A DRINK AND A SMOKE MYSELF.

HOW 'BOUT IT? ANYBODY ELSE? ON ME.

AN' HOW ABOUT YOU, BLUEJAY? GOT TIME TO BLOW WITH YER OL' UNCLE AND A REEKING STRANGER?

~ WHAT'S THE POINT O' WORKIN' HARD? WHAT'S THE POINT O' GAININ' RICHES? MONEY'S MEAN AN' BANKS ARE BITCHES ~ POVERTY'S ITS OWN REWARD ~

HAMADA

TIMES GONE BY, WE'D'A STUCK UP FOR THE WARDEN. NOW OL' GLAURIE, HE WAS A GOOD WARDEN ~ DI'NT MESS WITH GOOD BIZNESS BUT KEPT MARKET RULES. BUT THIS NEW KID, HE SHITS ON EV'-BODDY NO MATTA' WHAT & WHA' HAPP' TO OLD GLAURIE ~ HE WASH OKAY ~

WE DON'T KNOW, WHISKEY JACK YER TH' ONLY ONE OL' ENOUGH TO KNOW WHO TH' HELL YER TALKIN' ABOUT!

WELL, WHAT I HEARD WAS HE'D STILL BE ALIVE & WELL & JUMPING OUT OF BEDROOM WINDOWS IF IT WASN'T FOR ~

HEY!

YOU! YOU ~ YOU GET OUT OF HERE ~ THIS AIN'T NO PLACE FOR YOU ~ GET BACK OUT OF THIS BURNT PLACE ~ GET OUT ~ OUT ~ OUT

HEY, WHISKEY JACK ~

JACK'S GOIN' OFF AGAIN ~

IT'S NO PLACE FOR THE LIKES OF YOU, YOU HEAR ??

I'VE GOT BUSINESS HERE, YA CRAZY ~

BUSINESS? HA! WHAT YOU MEAN? A WOMAN?

~ I STILL KNOWS SOME STUFF ~ ~ OL' WISAKAJAC KNOWS ~ YOUR BLOOD'S FOLLOWING IN THE SECOND AIR, AND YOU DON'T HAVE A FUCKIN' CLUE ~ GET OUT ~ YOU CAN SO YOU SHOULD ~ DON'T LISTEN WHEN ALL THAT'S TALKIN' IS YER DICK ~

SORRY, HON. JACK DOESN'T MEAN ANY HARM REALLY... HE'S BEEN GOING DOWNHILL EVER SINCE THAT FEY-PLAGUE HIT HIM, BUT HE'S A GOOD OL' GUY USUALLY ~

~ FOX WENT OUT ON A SNOWY NIGHT ~ HE PRAYED TO THE MOON TO GIVE HIM LIGHT ~

HOW OFTEN DOES HE PROPHESY?

PFF! WHO CAN TELL?

BEHOLD, FRIENDS! SYMBOL OF OUR CITY OF ANVARD AND BELOVED CHILDREN'S FABLE HERE ELEGANTLY IMMORTALIZED! THE BLACK ANGEL!

HER SCULPTOR IS UNKNOWN, BUT IS NOW LARGELY BELIEVED TO HAVE BEEN RAEL UZENDERZO, THE LEGENDARY ICONOCLASSICIST. NOTE THAT HER HAIR AND FEATHERS ARE OF NATURALISTIC MATERIALS. OVER THE YEARS, THEY HAVE SUFFERED FROM EXPOSURE TO THE ELEMENTS —

HOW SO, YOU SAY? WITH THE CITY'S DOME TO PROTECT HER? WELL, FOLKS, THIS IS BECAUSE OUR ANGEL ACTUALLY PREDATES THE CONSTRUCTION OF THE DOME AND ITS SUPPORT STRUCTURE! YES, SHE'S THAT OLD!

—BUT OLDER STILL IS THE COLUMN ON WHICH SHE STANDS, WHICH, ALONG WITH THE RUINS YOU'LL SEE LATER ON OUR TOUR AND THE FORTIFIED LOOKOUT ATOP MOUNT CINO YOU SAW WHEN YOU CAME IN SIGHT OF THE CITY ARE PREHISTORIC, AND NO CONCLUSIVE DATE OF CONSTRUCTION HAS EVER BEEN AGREED UPON.

NOT TO WORRY, FOLKS— SHE HAS THE FINEST RECONSTRUCTION CREW POSSIBLE TO SEE TO HER EVERY NEED, CHAIRED BY PROFESSOR BRIGID JAVENSEN, OF ANVARD'S PRESTIGIOUS DJURAS COLLEGE.

SO,

THINK DON'T THINK

HAT A BUB BOBBA BLABBA FLABBA UB BUBBA BUB BL

??

!

12

LADIES AND GENTLEMEN, WHAT A PIECE OF LUCK!
OR RATHER, A PIECE OF OUR DOME! THE TECHNOLOGY THAT MADE OUR DOME AND ITS SUPPORT STRUCTURE IS NOW SADLY LOST. THE MATERIAL OF WHICH THE DOME IS MADE IS ENTIRELY UNKNOWN! ALTHOUGH IT ALLOWS VISIBLE LIGHT TO PENETRATE, IT APPEARS BLACK FROM ABOVE, AND IS OPAQUE TO ULTRAVIOLET AND CERTAIN OTHER FORMS OF RADIATION —

ALTHOUGH IT IS WELL KNOWN TO BE HARDER THAN DIAMOND OR CRYSTAL CERAMIC — OUR MOST SOPHISTICATED TOOLS CANNOT EVEN SCRATCH IT! — AND HAS RESISTED EARTHQUAKES OF INCREDIBLE MAGNITUDE WITH NO SIGNS OF DAMAGE, FOR SOME INSCRUTABLE REASON A FEW VERY LARGE HOLES HAVE APPEARED, AND OCCASIONALLY SMALL PIECES DO BREAK OFF—

HSSSFFFFF

FFHHSSSSS

AS YOU SEE, OUR REASEARCHERS ARE EVER-VIGILANT TO GLEAN WHATEVER DATA THEY CAN WHEN THIS HAPPENS — AND IT DOESN'T HAPPEN TWICE IN A YEAR, I ASSURE YOU!

OOP— AND THERE IT GOES!
SORRY, BOYS, YOU MIssED IT!

DISSOLUTION AFTER APPROXIMATELY NINETY-SEVEN SECONDS.

DEFINITE SIGNS OF REGROWTH ALONG LEADING EDGE.

FFFFFFFFFFFFFFF HHHH⊔⊔—

ALL SAMPLES UNSTABLE.

SO MUCH FOR "OH, MY HERO, HOW CAN I EVER REPAY YOU?"

OUR TOU[R]
AT THE BRI[DGE]
PROCEED D[...]
REACH [...]

SURE. IT'S ON THE RED LINE. SEE, ALL THE MAJOR TRAFFIC ROUTES ARE MARKED BY COLOR STRIPS. FOLLOW THE RED LINE **THAT** WAY NO MATTER HOW IT TWISTS & YOU'LL FIND THE TOWER PARK.

PEDESTRIAN RUSH-HOUR TRAFFIC IS MOVING RIGHT ALONG. ON TO VEHICULAR, HERE'S SPACEY KEN....

HO-**HO**!

WHERE'S YOUR LADY, COUSIN?

HAAAAHH~

OH!

HI, JAEGER!

HULSER, IT'S OKAY. HE'S OKAY. FRIEND, ALL RIGHT?

OGAY.

HI, ELLIE. WHAT'S WITH ALL THIS?

OH, WELL... WE'VE HAD A LOT OF ... TROUBLE LATELY. HIS ... OWNER, I GUESS, HIRED HIM OUT TO US AS A GUARD AND ANTI-THEPT, YOU KNOW?

FAR CRY FROM THE USUAL BOOKSTORE CAT, HUH?

HA HA! YES, I GUESS... BUT HE'S BEEN SO SWEET. REALLY, HIS HANDLER'S A LOT SCARIER THAN HE IS!

SPEAKING OF WHICH, WHERE'S MAN-HANDLER?

NOW IF ONLY HE HAD FUR...

EHHH...IF YOU MEAN ANN HANDLER, THE HEAD HONCHA~

..RRRIGHT BEHIND ME.

WHERE ELSE?

BEST VANTAGE POINT THERE IS. MAKES YOU LOOK AS IF YOU'RE ALWAYS LEAVING.

OOOWW!

GIVE BLOOD PLAY RUGBY

THEN I GUESS YOU WON'T WANT ME TO STAY LONG ENOUGH TO SHOW YOU THESE?

EEG~

HOW DO YOU FIND THESE? JEEZ—AAH, VISA GOLD, DIME-A-DOZEN--OH, WAIT, IT'S GOT A HOLOGRAM OF A RACCOON?? MAHAVIRA FIRST NATIONAL ~ WHO'D EVER THINK SO MANY DEFUNCT CREDIT CARDS WOULD STILL BE OUT THERE?

AHH, COLLECTOR'S MANIA ~

SO, YOUNGSTER, DID YOU HAVE A NICE WANDERING?

HEY, MISS LENNIE, I GOT YOUR ROCKS FOR YOU.

THAT'S LOVELY, DEAR. COME ON BACK INTO MY ROOM AND SHOW ME WHAT YOU'VE GOT.

OH, NOW, MISS LENNIE, I THOUGHT YOU'D NEVER ASK.

EEE HEE HEE! CHILD, YOU'D BETTER NOT BE ALL TALK WHEN I FINALLY CALL YOUR BLUFF!

YOU THINK I'M SCARED OF YOU BECAUSE YOU'RE NOT SEVENTEEN?

THAT WAS NICE, KID. BUT I'M STILL NOT CALLING YOUR BLUFF.

THAT'S THE GUY YOU'RE ALWAYS RAGGING ABOUT? HE DOESN'T SEEM SO BAD...

OH, HE CAN SLOP ON THE CHARM WHEN HE WANTS TO.

PSST—IT'S A PERSONALITY THING BETWEEN THEM. HER FAVORITE GAME IS "YOU CAN'T GET ONE UP ON ME" AND HIS IS "HOW MUCH CAN I GET AWAY WITH?"

IT'S WHAT MAKES HIM A MONSTER.

NOW, ANN...

I MEAN IT. HE IS ARROGANT... HE IS SHAMELESS, IMMORAL, ANTI-SOCIAL, IRRESPONSIBLE... HE'S TOO SLICK. HE'S SO CHARMING, BUT HE'S CALLOUS, CUNNING, AND TOO SELF-ASSURED. HE IS DANGEROUS. HE HAS AN EXPLOSIVE TEMPER, AND SOMEDAY IT IS GOING TO GO OFF BIG TIME. HE'S A PSYCHOPATH WAITING TO HAPPEN, AND SOMEDAY EVERYBODY WILL KNOW — —

AND THEN YOU'LL SAY YOU KNEW HIM WHEN, RIGHT?

OH, SHUT UP!

AH! WHAT A LOVELY PIECE OF AMBER!

IT'LL MAKE A FINE SUN-STONE.

D'I DO OKAY?

WELL, A GOOD SET OF GYLEH-STONES DEPENDS PARTLY ON HOW APPROPRIATE EACH STONE IS.

OBSIDIAN. NICELY POLISHED, TOO. SATURN FOR CERTAIN... ENDINGS. DRAWING INWARD —

SO — TIGER'S EYE? THIS MUST BE MY MARS STONE. ACTIVE, AGGRESSIVE, SOMETIMES DESTRUCTIVE...

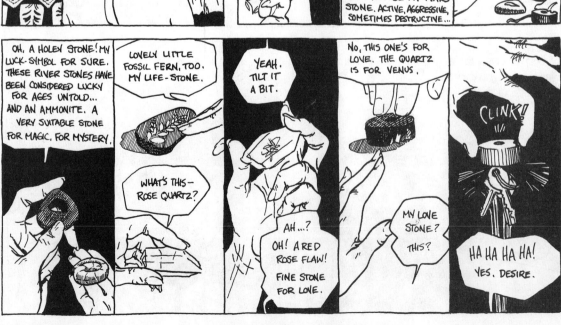

OH, A HOLEY STONE! MY LUCK-SYMBOL FOR SURE. THESE RIVER STONES HAVE BEEN CONSIDERED LUCKY FOR AGES UNTOLD... AND AN AMMONITE. A VERY SUITABLE STONE FOR MAGIC, FOR MYSTERY.

LOVELY LITTLE FOSSIL FERN, TOO. MY LIFE-STONE.

WHAT'S THIS — ROSE QUARTZ?

YEAH, TILT IT A BIT.

AH...? OH! A RED ROSE FLAW! FINE STONE FOR LOVE.

NO, THIS ONE'S FOR LOVE. THE QUARTZ IS FOR VENUS.

MY LOVE STONE? THIS?

CLINK!!

HA HA HA HA! YES. DESIRE.

THESE TWO... WHICH IS MY MOON?

THIS IS A SILVER MARK OF THE OLD EMPIRE — SEEN BETTER DAYS —

THAT'LL DO. WHAT'S LEFT?

THREE.

BUT THIS ONE, YOU CAN'T LET ANYBODY GET, CAUSE GOD KNOWS WHERE I'D FIND ANOTHER ONE. IT'S THE SAME STUFF AS THE DOME, BUT IT'S STABLE.

SO WHATTA YOU DO NOW?

JUPITER — THAT'S THIS BIG THREE-COLORED ONE —

WELL, SO HAS DAME MOON, THE HEMATITE?

THAT'S MERCURY.

NEWS — THIS DARK AND LIGHT STRIPY ONE.

MY HOME STONE, PRECIOUS BEYOND WORDS.

DO?

PUT 'EM BACK INTO THEIR PRETTY LITTLE LEATHER BAG, WHICH I *DID* NOTICE THAT YOU WERE SWEET ENOUGH TO MAKE FOR THEM, AND SETTLE ON A PRICE.

BUT AREN'T YOU GONNA USE THEM? I THOUGHT WHEN I GOT 'EM ALL BACK TO YOU THAT AT LEAST I'D GET MY FORTUNE TOLD.

NOO, NO. PURE RESEARCH, ALL OF THIS. DON'T FRET, I WON'T SELL THEM. MY CUSTOMERS CAN MAKE DO WITH CLAY TILES.

C'MON, MISS LENNIE —

EVERY KIND OF FORTUNE-TELLING THERE IS, YOU'VE GOT A BOOK ON IT, AND THE STUFF IT TAKES TO DO IT. YOU TELLIN' ME YOU DON'T ACTUALLY *DO* ANY OF THIS STUFF?

TRYING TO TELL ME YOU'RE NOT A WITCH?

ETHNOFOLKLORIST, IF YOU PLEASE. THIS IS MY RESEARCH. IF CHARGING A FEE FOR DEMONSTRATING THE MANY FORMS OF DIVINATION FURTHERS THAT RESEARCH, THEN THAT'S WHAT I DO.

THE REST IS SETTING, LOOKS TO IMPRESS MY CUSTOMERS, WHO COME TO BUY YI-JING STRAWS, TAROT CARDS, LEAF TEA, LEAD...

I BELIEVE YOU.

SELENE.

SELENE — **SELL**-UH-NEE

NOW.
HOW DID YOU GUESS MY NAME?

THE SIGN OUTSIDE...

"BOOKS, MUSIC, MISCELLANY". THERE'S A LOTTA MISCELLANEOUS STUFF IN HERE, BUT ONLY **ONE** MISS SELENE.

IT'S A HOLDOVER FROM WHEN IT WAS ILLEGAL, ISN'T IT? HIDING, PUTTING THINGS IN CODE.

WHAT YOU DO...

... WHAT YOU ARE ...

.. IS A FORM OF DIVINATION.

YOU'RE A GOOD TRACKER. A FINDER, AND THAT USED TO MEAN A LOT MORE THAN IT DOES TODAY.

IF YOU REALLY THINK HE'S SUCH A HORRIBLE PERSON, WHY DO YOU LET HIM HANG AROUND?

IF THERE'S A WASP IN THE ROOM, I WANT TO KEEP MY EYE ON IT.

GIVE BLOOD PLAY RUGBY

HEY, SO WHERE'S LYDIA? I FOUND A COPY OF THAT BOOK SHE WANTED.

SHE'S OFF TODAY.

WHAT BOOK?

FUMP!

"KNITTING WITH DOG HAIR". CAN I LEAVE IT HERE FOR 'ER?

SURE...

...IS THIS LEATHER?

GIVE BLOOD PLAY RUGBY

SIIGHH

NO, ACTUALLY, IT'S RAWHIDE, BUT **YES**, IT'S THE STOLEN FLESH OF ONE OF OUR ANIMAL BRETHREN, WHICH I NOT ONLY KILLED BUT ATE. WHAT ABOUT IT?

KILLING ANIMALS **IS ILLEGAL**--

NOW, GUYYS

DON'T FREAK OUT, GUYS. WHAT'S DONE IS DONE, RIGHT?

RETURN THE DEAD TO THE SOIL, RIGHT?

RIGHT.

SO....!

BEATS HELL OUT OF FLUSHING IT DOWN THE JANE TO RETURN IT TO THE SEA, DOESN'T IT?

" A NEEDLE PULLING THREAD ... "

GIVE BLOO PLAY

CAUGHT YOUR ACT DOWN AT THE FREE MARKET. SIGN HERE.

'TH' HELL IS IT?

GIVE PLA

IT'S AN ASSOCIATION FOR THE RIGHTS OF INDIGENOUS PEOPLE. I'M SURE YOU'LL WANT TO SHOW YOUR SUPPORT OF THEIR RECLAIMING THEIR LAND.

GIVE

AIN'T NO SUCH THING AS INDIGENOUS. IT ALL COMES DOWN TO PUSH AND SHOVE OVER TERRITORY.

YOU'RE REALLY **NOT** TRIBAL, ARE YOU?

I'M TOLD YOU'VE BEEN PASSING YOURSELF OFF AS INDIAN FOR YEARS.

YEAH. WELL, **I'M** TOLD THAT THERE AIN'T A LESBIAN ALIVE WHO DOESN'T **REALLY** WANT TO SUCK COCK.

PLIK!

"BEHOLD THE GREAT MAD RIVER! OR AT LEAST ITS IMAGE ON VIDEO, AS IT'S NOT ADVISED TO GET TOO CLOSE TO THE WATER. MANY RIVERS HAVE BEEN CALLED 'RED' BUT AS YOU CAN SURELY SEE, NONE HAVE EVER BEEN SO EMINENTLY QUALIFIED.

"HOW MANY RIVERS IN MYTH AND IN HISTORY HAVE BEEN SAID TO RUN RED WITH BLOOD? WITH WHOSE BLOOD DOES OUR MIGHTY DELTA RUN, TO GIVE IT SUCH A LIVID TINGE?"

"THE SEA'S A LOVELY LADY, IF YOU PLAY *IN* HER. IF YOU PLAY *WITH* HER, SHE IS A *BITCH!*"

"~ THIS IS PIRATE STATION 622 BRINGING YOU THE HOURLY NIGHT-LIFE HAZARD SPOT REPORT, COVERING ALL THIRTY-TWO BOROUGHS OF THE CITY.
UPPER AND LOWER AVENTINE ARE QUIET BUT TENSE - SNOB HILL'S JUST SLOPPIN' OVER WITH RENT-A-COPS LOOKIN' FOR RAISES—

"~ TOURIST JAMPACK AT BAEDEKER'S, SO STEER CLEAR OR BY-GOD BE PHOTOGRAPHED. EVER SINCE THIS CLUB WAS PUT ON THE CIVIC WALKING TOUR IT'S LOOKED LIKE THE METRO OUTTA TOWN ON GODZILLA TWO-FOR-ONE DAY - SHIT, LADY——

"— PRETTY QUIET ALL THROUGH IMBRIUM. SLIGHT VEHICULAR DETOUR AROUND A GANG RUMBLE BETWEEN HARSKAE AND A GANG OF RUSALKAS NEW TO THE BOROUGH. COUPLE STREET FESTS WARMING UP FOR LAESKE RUNNING SEASON ~

"— CHYERNY HAS AN UNUSUAL AMOUNT OF FOOT TRAFFIC TONIGHT, DIRECTLY RESULTING FROM HIGH TIDE IN SWINE LAGOON. BIG-TIME STANDING ON ALL MAJOR STREETS AND WALKWAYS, SO WE'RE WATCHIN' CLOSE FOR THE INEVITABLE RIOTING AS FUMES FROM THE RIVER DO WHAT THEY DO BEST~

"~ CHEMICAL SPILL FROM LOCAL FAST-FOOD HAS EMPTIED OUT MOST OF JORAN. THE ARENA, HOWEVER, IS STILL GOIN' STRONG AS ALWAYS, SO IF YOU'VE GOT A SEAL-SUIT OR THE CASH FOR A SURROGATE, COME ON DOWN!

"~ DOWN IN GULLAHINGLA WE HAVE A SPECTACULAR BAR-FIGHT TAKING PLACE IN THE GODSFEAST TAVERN~ ~IT'S PRESUMED TO BE OVER A WOMAN BUT THIS IS UNCONFIRMED ~ OVER THREE THOUSAND HOURS OF DAMAGE HAVE ALREADY BEEN DONE ~

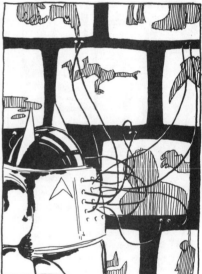

26

SPANGG

SCREEEE BAM

FOR GODDESS' SAKE, CHANGE THE CHANNEL. I CAN'T HANDLE ANY MORE CARNAGE TONIGHT.

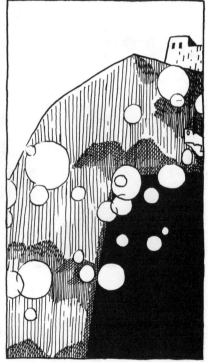

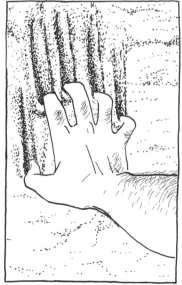

BETTER MAKE IT A QUICKIE, SISTER. YE OL' YELLA SCHOOL BUS DOTH APPROACH.

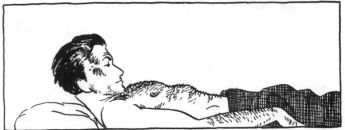

EXCUSE ME.

I MUST NOW KILL MY OWN FLESH AND BLOOD.

PHOO

GOD DAMN HEART BREAKER ...

TAP TAP TAP TAP

CAR, MOM. THINK WHEELS.

TUBE PASS, RACHEL. THINK CYLINDER.

mmf.

34

WELL, YOU LOOK MUCH BETTER TODAY.

YEAH... I ALWAYS DID BOUNCE BACK QUICK.

I DECLARE, IT'S AMAZING HOW A GOOD NIGHT'S SLEEP CAN BRING UP YOUR COLOR.

YOU'RE RAISING A DRAGON, EMMA.

HA HA HA HAA—

HEE HEE HEH!

SNORT!

NOO, NO. IT'S A PHASE. BELIEVE IT OR NOT, SHE'S STILL A VIRGIN, AND SHE'S TESTING THE WATERS. DOING "DANGEROUS" THINGS, YOU KNOW?

SHE'LL CALM DOWN.

NNGH~

SO ... BIG FIGHT OR LITTLE ONE?

EHH·~ MIDDLING.

ANYBODY LOOKING FOR YOU?

I DON'T KNOW.

I CAN'T HELP BUT WORRY ABOUT YOU, BUT I DON'T KNOW WHY... YOU ALWAYS COME IN LOOKING LIKE SOMETHING EVEN AN EMERGENCY ROOM COULDN'T HANDLE, BUT WHEN I WASH YOU OFF IT'S NEVER AS BAD AS I'D IMAGINED....

MMF... STILL... I'D LIKE YOU TO STAY A ... UM. FEW DAYS. HOWEVER LONG YOU WANT... REALLY... TILL I KNOW YOU'RE OKAY...

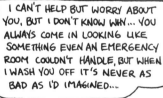

MM— NOW— I'M SURE YOU'RE JUST **STARVED** OF FEMALE COMPANY—

ALTHOUGH I EXPECT MY GIRL RACHEL'S MORE YOUR TASTE.

MY REPUTATION'S GETTING OUT OF HAND.

I'LL SAY.

CAN I HELP IT IF THE ONLY WOMEN WHO EVER MAKE PASSES AT **ME** ARE TEEN-AGERS?

A YOUNG GIRL JUST OUT OF HER CHANGE IS BEAUTIFUL.... BUT A FULL-BLOWN WOMAN IS LOVELY TOO..., AND AN OLD WOMAN TOO. WOMEN ARE ALWAYS ON THEIR WAY TO BEING SOMETHING ELSE... THAT'S WHAT I LOVE. MEN NEVER CHANGE. I DON'T KNOW WHAT **YOU** SEE IN **US.**

HM. THERE'S AN OLD MIDDLE KINGDOM BLESSING THAT GOES SOMETHING LIKE "MAY YOUR SONS BE MANY AND STRONG AND UGLY AND YOUR DAUGHTERS BE FEW AND LOVELY".

=SNAP=

MMM... MAY YOUR DAUGHTERS BE MANY AND STRONG AND LOVELY AND DON'T BOTHER WITH THE SONS A'TALL...

NOW **REALLY**, YA YOUNG FIRE HOSE— I GOTTA GO TO A SITE. WILL YOU BE OKAY WITH MARCIE HERE?

SURE —— WHY NOT?

SHE'S GOT SOME KIND OF BUG. DON'T YOU USUALLY GET THE HORRORS AROUND SICK PEOPLE?

AW, FER— AS IF I COULDN'T TAKE CARE OF HER —SHE'S LIKE MY SISTER— WELL, IF YOU **WERE** HER BROTHER AND YOU STILL VANISHED FOR MONTHS OR YEARS WITH NO WORD—

EMMA— —I WOULDN'T THINK YOU'D HAVE THE NERVE TO LOOK SURPRISED YOU'D MISSED A FEW THINGS—

—EMMA—

...SIGH....

ALL RIGHT... ALL RIGHT.

SOMETIMES I'M JUST NOT SURE WHAT YOU NEED FROM US, LOVE.

...THURSDAY'S CIVIL-SERVANT DEATH TOLL INCLUDES LESTER ANTHONY SOFFIT, MARKET WARDEN OF MUNICIPAL FREE MARKET FIFTEEN. WARDEN SOFFIT WAS KILLED WHILE OFF-DUTY IN A FIVE-LEVEL FALL FROM THE GODSFEAST TAVERN. HE WAS FIFTY-ONE——

CLICK

CLICK!

IT'S TIME FOR SAWING FOR TEENS

LAVEAU'S
BOOKS • MUSIC • MISCELLAN

AU'S

OF AN EVENING, SISTERS—

UM.

EVENING.

OOH... WHOOZA SHWEETIE? BEEN EARNING YOUR KEEP? AMANNO HURAGA'AHE—

FULA AMA'HARAH— RAMALLAH NAAM AYO A'GOBAYEH—

HOW'S HE BEEN? PROVED USEFUL?

OH, UH, SURE—

WELL, YES AND NO.

OH?

YES, IN THAT EVERYONE'S ON THEIR BEST BEHAVIOR SINCE WE'VE HAD HIM. UNDERSTAND, IT WAS NEVER OUR CUSTOMERS WHO WERE THE PROBLEM—

ANN, HE'S CAUGHT EIGHT SHOPLIFTERS. FORMER REGULARS.

TRUE, BUT THE REAL PROBLEM WAS THE PERSISTENT HOLDUPS AND BREAK-INS.

AND HATE CRIMES.

38

IT ISN'T AS IF HE HASN'T PREVENTED THAT SORT OF THING. QUITE WELL, IN FACT. BUT SUCH A LARGE ANIMAL IS A CROWD-DRAW, AND WE'VE HAD A LOT MORE FRINGE TYPES SINCE WE HIRED HIM.

... AND YOU CAN'T DENY THAT YOU YOURSELF ARE A SOURCE OF CURIOSITY.

COUPLE BIZARROS HAVE TRIED TO GET IN TOUCH WITH YOU THROUGH US.

SO?

I CAN'T BE BOTHERED WITH SUCH FOOLISHNESS. NOR, I PRESUME, CAN YOU. ARE YOU REFUSING HULGER'S HIRE?

≡HAH≡ NO, NOT YET. I'LL SWAP OLD WEIRDOS FOR NEW, FOR NOW.

GOOD. THE MONEY'S BEEN WELCOME. EVEN FULL SCHOLAR-SHIPS DON'T PROVIDE THAT MUCH FOOD MONEY.

NEVER UNDERESTIMATE THE ENTERTAINMENT VALUE OF ECCENTRICITY—

HEY, WHO'S THIS LITTLE GUY? I DIDN'T KNOW YOU HAD TWO!

AH, THIS IS JINGKO. COME IN, SHY BOY.

THERE'S ALSO A THIRD, KOHUT. HE'S MY OTHER REASON FOR HIRING HULGER OUT. HULGER'S A RECENT ADDITION, AND THEY TWO HAVEN'T SETTLED WHO'S TO BE TOP CAT.

—OR DANGER—

HAS TO BE SETTLED. BUT AFTER FINALS.

THREE? GOOD GODDESS, THAT MUST BE EXPENSIVE!

WHY DO YOU, ANYWAY? REALLY— NOBILITY OR NOT, ISN'T IT SELF-INDULGENT TO KEEP SUCH EXTRAVAGANT PETS?

YOU MIS-UNDERSTAND US.

MY ULUHAKA— MY FOUR-LEGGED ONES— ARE NOT MY PETS. HULGER IS MY GRANDMOTHER'S BROTHER. KOHUT IS MY COUSIN. AND JINGKO— JINGKO IS MY SON.

SO.... THERE REALLY ARE — MALE NYIMA?

DON'T BE SILLY.

IF THOSE ARE THE MALES — UNCLE, COUSIN, SON —

— THEN WHO'S HER HUSBAND?

HEY, DEMON SEED.

MY-OH, WHAT A SHORT SCHOOL DAY.

OR IS IT JUST THAT YOU'RE SO BRILLIANT THAT YOU JUST SUCKED THE INSTITUTION DRY OF KNOWLEDGE IN HALF THE TIME AND NOW YOU'VE GOT NO REASON EVER TO GO BACK?

SO I HAD A FEW ERRANDS TO RUN.

YOU DON'T LOOK SO GOOD.

I DON'T FEEL SO GOOD.

YOU DON'T LOOK LIKE YOU FEEL SO GOOD.

WELL, I DON'T FEEL LIKE I LOOK LIKE I FEEL SO GOOD.

YOU DON'T LOOK LIKE YOU FEEL LIKE YOU LOOK LIKE YOU FEEL SO GOOD.

YEAH, WELL, I DON'T FEEL LIKE I LOOK LIKE I FEEL LIKE I LOOK LIKE I FEEL SO GOOD.

WELL, I'M SORRY YOU DON'T FEEL LIKE YOU LOOK LIKE YOU FEEL LIKE YOU LOOK LIKE YOU FEEL SO GOOD.

OH, WELL, I'M SORRY I DON'T FEEL LIKE I LOOK LIKE I FEEL LIKE I LOOK LIKE I FEEL SO GOOD.

I'M DEEPLY CONCERNED ABOUT YOUR SYMPATHY WITH MY EMPATHY OVER OUR COMMON PERCEPTION OF THE DETERIORATION OF YOUR GENERAL APPEARANCE AND PRESUMABLY SIMILARLY DEFICIENT HEALTH! AAAGH!

HEY, LAY OFF THE HITTING! I DON'T FEEL SO GOOD.

"YE HAVE ALL SINNED..." "YEASS~" BUT WHICH ONE OF YOU CAN SAY AS I CAN SAY THAT YOU DROVE A GOOD MAN TO MURDER "OOGHH" CAUSE I KEPT A-HOUNDIN' HIM FOR PERFUME AND CLOTHES AND FACE PAINT "OOOUHHH"~ AN-AND HE SLEW TWO HUMAN BEINGS AND HE COME TO ME AND SAID TAKE THIS MONEY AND BUY YOURSELF THE CLOTHES AND THE PAINT ~ BUT BRETHREN - BROTHER — THAT'S WHERE THE LORD STEPPED IN ——"

"NOW WEREN'T YOU AFRAID, LITTLE LAMBS, DOWN THERE IN ALL THAT DARK?"

KID... WHY IN THE HELL ARE WE WATCHING THIS MESS?

ARE YOU KIDDING? THIS IS A GREAT MOVIE.

NOW LEMME SEE IF I'VE GOT THIS STRAIGHT—

IT'S HARD TIMES. THESE TWO KIDS, THEIR DADDY GOT DESPERATE AND STOLE A BUNCHA MONEY, KNOWING HE COULDN'T GET AWAY. HE HIDES IT WITH HIS KIDS AND MAKES THEM SWEAR ON THEIR COMMON BLOOD NOT TO TELL.

COPS COME AND TAKE HIM AWAY, AND HE'S TO DIE. WHILE HE'S IN GAOL THIS OTHER MAN, WHO PREYS ON SAD LONELY WOMEN, FINDS OUT ABOUT ALL THIS AND AS SOON AS THE DAD IS DEAD SETS OFF TO GET THAT MONEY.

NOW THIS MAN, HE'S A PREACHER, BUT HE'S CRAZY—HE LOOKS AT A WOMAN, HE SEES A DEVIL. HE GOES TO THIS WOMAN, THE MOTHER, AND WORMS HIS WAY INTO HER, BUT MARRY HER OR NOT HE WON'T TOUCH HER. HE JUST WORKS ON HER, SHARPENS HER SORROW AND GUILT.

AND THE SON SEES THROUGH HIM, AND SO HE TURNS MOTHER AGAINST HER SON. THE LITTLE ONE, SHE'S TOO LITTLE TO SEE HIM FOR WHAT HE IS. SHE WANTS A DADDY.

SO THE WOMAN COMES TO SEE THAT THE PREACHER MAN'S A RATTLE-SNAKE, AND HE KILLS HER AND IT'S CLEAR SHE THINKS SHE'S EARNED IT.

SO NOW THE BOY HAS TO RUN AWAY WITH HIS SISTER, NOW HIS ONLY BLOOD, DOWN THE RIVER ROAD, ALONE UNDER THAT BONE MOON, WITH THAT TWIST-HEAD RIGHT AFTER THEM?

NO, KID. UH-UH. I CAN'T WATCH THIS.

BIG OL' BUTCH THING LIKE YOU, AND YOU GET THE SQUEALS OVER A MOVIE—

WOULD IT HELP YOU TO KNOW THAT IT ALL ENDS IN A SICKENINGLY HAPPY, CATHARTIC WAY?

NO. SHIT LIKE THIS HAPPENS EVERY DAY. IF I CHANCE TO TRIP OVER IT, I CAN TRY TO DO SOMETHING ABOUT IT. I DON'T WANNA THINK ABOUT IT IF IT AIN'T REAL. JUST MAKES ME TENSE.

NOW HERE WE GO.

"YOU'RE GONNA JUMP ON ME!"
"HUH?"
"YOU'RE GONNA JUMP ON ME! LIKE NERO JUMPED ON POPEIA!"
"WHO?!?"

HUH.

TEEK TOCK
TEEK TOCK
TEEK TOCK
···...

' THIS TIME THE GROUND ITSELF HAD REARED UP AND DESTROYED WHAT WAS HIS.
"LOOKY HERE," IT SAID. "YOU AIN'T MORE'N A BUG T' ME...YOU GAVE UP MOST EVERYTHING T' GO A-ROVING ...HOME, FRIENDS, WIFELY COMFORTS, JUST TO BE FREE.
"WELL, NOW I'VE TOOK THE REST AND YOUR FREEDOM'S A DRUNKARD'S DREAM, CAUSE YOU BELONG T' **ME**."

'SECH WERE THE THINGS THE GROUND WHISPERED TO HIM AND MACAUSTAIRE WAS INCLINED TO TAKE IT PERSONAL.'

PSSH—

FUMP!

HEY, MARS --

WHAT'S WRONG, SIS?

I'M SICK.

I KNOW, I MEAN WHAT'S THE MATTER?

MAMA SEES IT.

SHE **SEES** IT, BUT SHE DOESN'T BELIEVE IT. SHE JUST THINKS YOU WEREN'T EVER REALLY HURT BAD. BUT YOU **WERE**.

YES, KID. I WAS.

IT'S JUST THE WAY I AM, MARCIE.

IF I **DON'T** GET HURT, IT'S WORSE FOR ME.

BUT I DON'T WANT YOU TO BE AFRAID OF ME.

THAT'S JUST WHAT DADDY USED TO SAY. THAT HE DIDN'T WANT US TO BE SCARED.

BUT MAMA SAYS HE DID REALLY.

HOW VERY BRONTË ESQUE. LITTLE SISTER IS DEVELOPING QUITE THE DRAMATIC FLAIR, NO?

THOUGH I'LL TELL YOU, I'LL TAKE *HER* DRAMAS OVER RRRACHEL'S ANY DAY.

HOW'S THAT BROKEN COLLARBONE, BY THE WAY?

FINE.

CRACKED CHEEKBONE? CONCUSSION?

FINE.

NOT TO MENTION SOME CRACKED RIBS, MULTIPLE LACERATIONS, AND A FEW LOST TEETH?

WOULD YOU CARE IF I TOLD YOU I TOOK PICTURES OF YOU AFTER MOM WENT TO BED?

EASY ENOUGH TO TAKE MORE OF YOU AS YOU ARE TODAY FOR COMPARISON.

GIRL, THE FRICKIN' ARMY HAS TIME-LAPSE MOVIES OF ME DOING WHAT AIN'T ANYTHING SPECIAL TO ME. I'LL GO GET MY COPIES, WE'LL RUN 'EM BACKWARDS, LOADS O' LAUGHS.

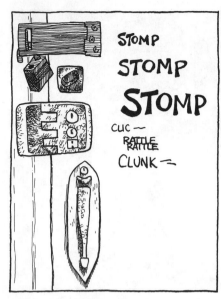

STOMP
STOMP
STOMP
CLIC —
RATTLE
RATTLE
CLUNK —

WELP— MAIN FLOOR, EVERYBODY OFF —

MM.

GRRR~

SLAM
CLINKITY CLAK~

THOSE DAMNED IF-DEER! I SPEND TWENTY WEEKS WORKING ON THIS SPREAD, AND JUST AS I'VE FINALLY COAXED THE ROSES INTO BLOOM, THOSE FETID THINGS ATE ALL OF THE BUDS!

SO PUT TOBACCO WHEREVER YOU DON'T WANT THEM TO GO. ALL DEER HATE THAT.

OH, WELL, FINE! I HATE IT, TOO!

NO, NO, FRIZZIE. I MEAN LIVE TOBACCO PLANTS. WHO'D KNOW? JUST ANOTHER BIG BROADLEAFED ORNAMENTAL PLANT.

AND IT'S WHAT, DEER REPELLANT?

YUP.

THANKS, HONEY. NOW ALL I GOTTA DO IS FIND SOMEBODY WHO CAN SELL ME — EMMA~ WHAT THE HELL DID BRIGHAM DO TO THAT KID TO MAKE HER SO FLINCHY?

IT WASN'T JUST TO HER.

IT'S JUST HARDER FOR MARCELLA TO LET GO OF, SINCE SHE WAS BORN TO IT. IT'S THE ONLY LIFE SHE KNEW.

"WE **WERE** LIVING IN A WAR ZONE. HE TOLD US THAT WE WERE IN DANGER... WHAT REASON DID I HAVE TO DISBELIEVE HIM?"

"IT'S SO EASY TO BE AFRAID WHEN YOU HAVE CHILDREN.

"BRIGHAM...

"I'LL NEVER KNOW WHEN HE STARTED NEEDING OUR FEAR...

"FEEDING IT.

"HE WAS A CAPTAIN, AFTER ALL. HE KNEW WHAT WAS GOING ON. **REALLY** GOING ON. HE ALWAYS LET US KNOW WE WERE HEARING PRIVILEGED INFORMATION.

BIT BY BIT HE WHITTLED AWAY OUR FREEDOM.

"FIRST IT'S DON'T GO OUT ALONE AT NIGHT, LOCK YOUR DOOR. THEN IT'S DON'T GO OUT AT NIGHT AT ALL. LOCK YOUR DOOR DURING THE DAY TOO.

"THEN IT'S SLEEP IN THE MARBLE BATHTUB, IN CASE SOMEONE SHOOTS THROUGH THE WALLS OF THE HOUSE. DON'T GO OUT EVEN IN DAYLIGHT WITHOUT AN ARMED ESCORT — BRIG, OF COURSE, SINCE HE DIDN'T TRUST THE OTHER SOLDIERS OR OFFICERS ANYMORE.

"BUT HE WOULDN'T TAKE US AWAY FROM THE DANGER.

RACHEL... SUCH A LITTLE GIRL... MAKING CROWNS AND NECKLACES OUT OF SPENT SHELL CASINGS...

"HE NEVER HIT US.

"NEVER DID ANYTHING OVERTLY THREATENING.

"BUT EVERYTHING HE DID WAS CALCULATED TO MAKE US AFRAID, SO WE'D CLING TO OUR ONLY PROTECTOR.

"THE DANGER **WAS** REAL, AT FIRST... IT MUST HAVE BEEN, THAT BATTLE ZONE IS IN NEWS RECORDS... BUT BY THE TIME I LEFT HIM, I FOUND THAT THE FIGHTING HAD BEEN OVER FOR FOUR YEARS."

I'LL NOT FORGET MY TRIP OUT VERY SOON... OR MY LIFE WITH HIM.

EVEN NOW—WHEN YOU CAME IN HERE LAST NIGHT LOOKING HALF KILLED—EVEN THOUGH I KNOW HE'S IN A MILITARY PRISON I STILL THOUGHT IT MUST HAVE BEEN BRIG WHO'D BEATEN YOU SO TERRIBLY—

WHY DIDN'T YOU TELL ME, MOM?

YOU?

WHAT COULD YOU HAVE DONE? YOU WEREN'T AN OFFICER. YOU WERE JUST A KID, AND ON A CONVICT BILLET AT THAT.

BESIDES, YOU WERE IN THE V.A. HOSPITAL FOR SO LONG, WE NEVER EVEN KNEW WHEN YOU GOT OUT. AND THEN, HOW COULD WE HAVE FOUND YOU?

OKAY, OKAY...

WHEN DID YOU WAKE UP, ANYWAY?

OH, MOM—

WHAT ARE YOU DOING HOME THIS TIME?

NORMALLY I'D NEVER BLOW MY COVER, BUT MARCIE ISN'T BREATHING.

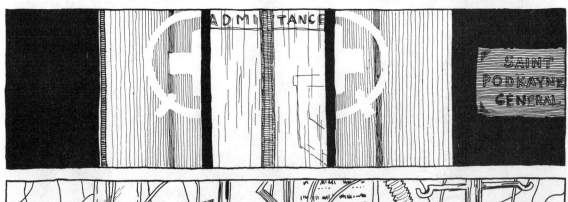

ADMITTANCE

SAINT PODKAYNE GENERAL

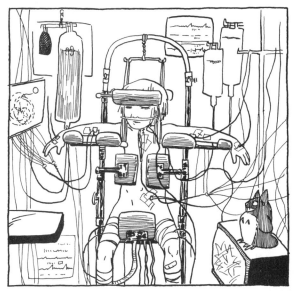

IF YOU'RE GOING TO BE SICK, GO BACK TO THE WAITING ROOM.

BORETUM

I KNOW THESE ANGEL-FRAMES DON'T LOOK GOOD, SIR, BUT BELIEVE ME, IT'S THE BEST THING FOR YOUR LITTLE GIRL—

PLEASE HAVE AS MANY FORMS OF I.D. AS HUMANLY POSSIBLE READY AT ALL TIMES

HUL=
=URGH=
HUK=HUK=
BLAAH=
ULK=
EGA UHHH=
BUICK! BUICK! BUICK!

MOANN ~~......

BOA ♪

=HAAHH=

GOD. THAT HOSPITAL SMELL---

OH, WELL, THE AROMA OUT HERE IS MUCH IMPROVED.

CONFESS, MY LAD. PURGE THE SOUL AS WELL AS THE BODY. WHY DO YOU SO HATE HOSPITALS? IT'S NOT AS IF YOU HAVE ANY USE FOR THEM.

"FALL OF THE YEAR I MET YOU GUYS... HURT MY HEAD. YOU **KNOW** WHAT IT TAKES TO REALLY HURT ME.

I DON'T KNOW WHY, BUT I DIDN'T COME BACK OUT OF IT. THE DAMAGE HEALED. BUT I DIDN'T WAKE UP. GODDAMN ARMY DOCTORS.... "

"HOW LONG WERE YOU COMATOSE ? "

"ELEVEN MONTHS. MAYBE IT WAS ALL THE JUNK THEY MUST'VE BEEN PUTTING INTO ME, I DON'T KNOW. "

"BUT ARMY HOSPITALS DON'T KEEP SERVICE-MEN ON LIFE SUPPORT MORE THAN SIX WEEKS."

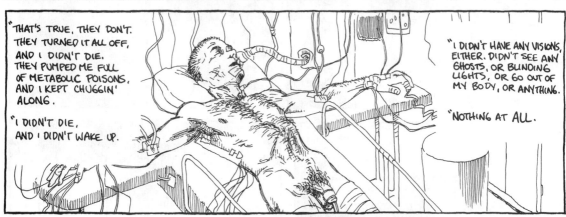

"THAT'S TRUE, THEY DON'T. THEY TURNED IT ALL OFF, AND I DIDN'T DIE. THEY PUMPED ME FULL OF METABOLIC POISONS, AND I KEPT CHUGGIN' ALONG.

"I DIDN'T DIE, AND I DIDN'T WAKE UP.

"I DIDN'T HAVE ANY VISIONS, EITHER. DIDN'T SEE ANY GHOSTS, OR BLINDING LIGHTS, OR GO OUT OF MY BODY, OR ANYTHING.

"NOTHING AT ALL.

"ALL I REMEMBER IS BEING THIRSTY...

I'D SEE PEOPLE... DOCTORS, NURSES, MY BUDDIES... I'D BEG 'EM FOR WATER, BUT IT WAS LIKE IN DREAMS WHERE YOU CAN'T TALK, OR IF YOU CAN, YOU CAN'T SPEAK ANY LANGUAGE PEOPLE UNDERSTAND.... "

"WHAT WOKE YOU UP ? "

"THEY STOPPED FEEDING ME... AFTER A WHILE THAT GOT ME OUT OF BED.

"AND A WHILE AFTER THAT I WOKE UP. "

I HATE NOT KNOWING WHAT TO DO NEXT, GIRL.

I'M GOING NOW.

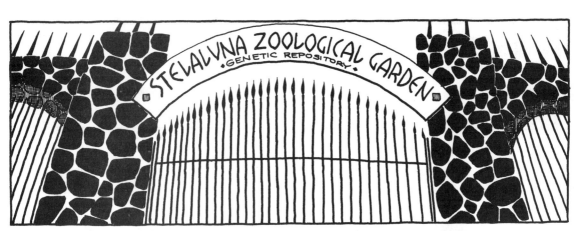

RELAX, MAN. I'M OUT.

4-LEGGED
TWO-LEGGED
NO-LEGGED
MULTIPLE
CONCESSION

GREATER NORTHERN BLANKET HOG

LOOK, JERKY, I DON'T KNOW WHAT KINDA CRAZED INSURANCE SCAM YER TRYINA PULL HERE, BUT **YOU** STAY TH' **GODDAMNED HELL AWAY** FROM MY ANIMALS!

YOU DON'T SEEM TO REALIZE THESE ARE **REAL** PREDATORS! HAVE YOU EVER **SEEN** AN ANIMAL MAULING?

NO, OF COURSE YOU HAVEN'T — PROBABLY NEVER EVEN SET FOOT OUT OF THIS NICE SAFE LITTLE CITY —

BUSTER, **YOU** DON'T SEEM TO REALIZE THAT THERE'S A **BIIIG** DIFFERENCE BETWEEN **WILD** ANIMALS AND THESE BORED, FAT ZOO-BRED VEGETABLES.

THAT'S ANOTHER THING!

YOU COULD BE CARRYING GOD KNOWS WHAT VIRUSES! THOSE ANIMALS ARE RARE AND HARD TO BREED, AND **VERY** SUSCEPTIBLE ~~

HEY, MAN, MAKE UP YOUR MIND --

ARE **THEY** A DANGER TO ME, OR AM I A DANGER TO **THEM**?

IT DOESN'T MATTER -- THE ZOO'S CLOSED, YOU'RE OUTTA LINE, AND YOU'RE **OUT!**

OKAY, OKAY, FINE. BUT MAN, YOU'VE GOT TO REALIZE THAT THOSE ARE **NOT** REAL PREDATORS.

HELL THEY'RE NOT!

NO, THEY'RE NOT. THEY'RE BORED SUBURBANITES.

ATTITUDES LIKE YOURS GET PEOPLE **KILLED** EVERY DAY! JUST YESTERDAY SOME GADDAMN TOURIST GOT THE CRAP STOMPED OUT OF 'ER WALKIN' UP TO A RAY-DEER --

-- TRY'NA TAKE A PICTURE WITH IT FER CHRISSAKES -- SO **INSTEAD** OF TELLIN' HER SHE'S A MORON WHO GOT OFF LIGHT WITH JUST STITCHES AN A CONCUSSION, THE CITY'S GOTTA HUNT THE ANIMAL DOWN AND KILL IT! **LIKE** THEY'LL ACTUALLY **FIND** THE EXACT SAME DEER --

HEY, I NEVER SAID SUBURBANITES CAN'T FIGHT BACK. **I** WOULDN'T GET BETWEEN THEM 'N THEIR REMOTE CONTROLS. LEMME GET THAT FOR YA --

WHAT I'M SAYIN' IS, IT TAKES MORE THAN CLAWS, TEETH, OR EVEN INSTINCT TO MAKE A PREDATOR.

REAL PREDATORS ARE OPPORTUNISTS, CAN'T AFFORD TO MISS A CHANCE.

CLANG!

HEY!

54

CRAK! CRUNCH CRUNCH

CRIK CRUK

HAVIN' TROUBLE?

UH — YEAH. WON'T START, AND I'M LATE.

AN' LOOKS LIKE YER GONNA BE LATER. LEMME TAKE A LOOK— I USETA WORK ON THESE THINGS.

HERE'S YOUR PROBLEM— REACH IN HERE —

WHERE?

WAY THE HELL DOWN IN THERE. IT'S A LOOSE WIRE. GOT IT?

YEAH ... YEAH, I GOT IT!

DAMNEDEST THING, TOO— THIS HEAP STARTED UP JUST **FINE** WHEN I DROVE IT HERE YESTERDAY.

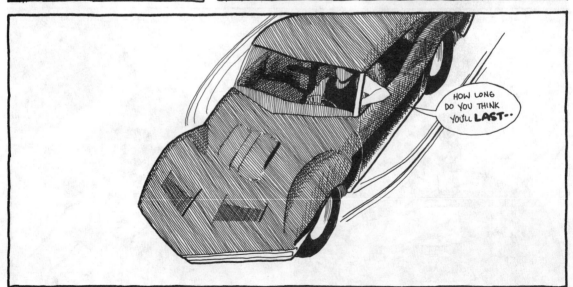

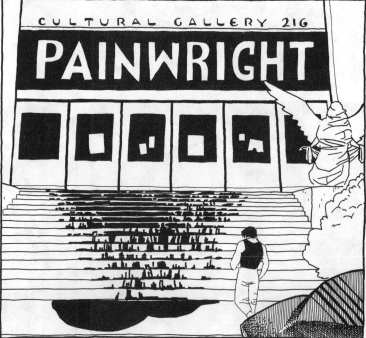

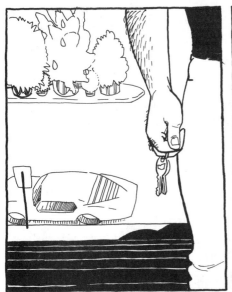

CLOSED
جزئ · AIYAO · ✳
HOURS
DRAGON HOUR
TO
RAT HOUR
DAY SHIFT AND
MIDNIGHT SHIFT

SHIT.

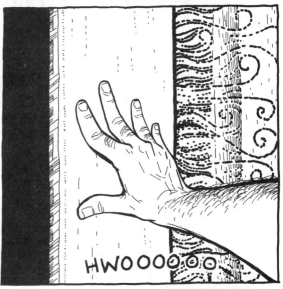

HWOOOOOO

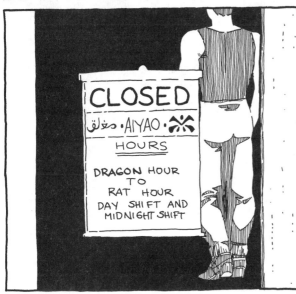

CLOSED
جزئ · AIYAO · ✳
HOURS
DRAGON HOUR
TO
RAT HOUR
DAY SHIFT AND
MIDNIGHT SHIFT

IT WAS CLOSED,
BUT NOT LOCKED,
SO I WENT IN.

IT'S BEEN AGES
SINCE I SET FOOT
IN THIS WEIRD
OLD BARN.

LOST
"FLUFFY"
REWARD $$!!
NO QUESTIONS ASKED

"THE PAINWRIGHT GALLERY".
MUSEUM OF PAIN. EVERY-
THING FROM PAPER CUTS TO
THE DEATH OF A THOUSAND CUTS.

IF IT'S TO DO WITH
PAIN, IT'S IN HERE.

≡HHAAHH≡

I HAVE A QUESTION.

FLIK!

FIRST I WANT TO SEE THE TESTAMENT OF EMMA MARLENA GROSVENOR.

CHNK--

61

INFORMATION IS OUR CURRENCY.

YOU KNOW OUR PRICE.

ALL RIGHT. FINE.

THE WORST THING THAT EVER HAPPENED TO ME. AND THE THING I'M MOST AFRAID OF.

THE DEATH OF MY FATHER.

I'M **SURE** HE WAS MY FATHER.

CRIK

DO I HAVE OTHER FAMILY?

WHY AM I THE WAY I AM?

BUT THE ROTTEN OLD FUCK DIED, AND I GOT NOBODY ELSE TO ASK.

NOW.

EMMA.

FSSK!

NO PARKING EVER EVER EVER EVER

I'M HERE BECAUSE I'VE BEEN TOLD THAT THERE ARE ONLY TWO THERAPIES FOR-- FOR ME.

I CAN'T AFFORD MASSAGE, SO I'M TELLING MY STORY.

MY STORY WASN'T SUPPOSED TO BE LIKE THIS ...

OH, SHE 'UZ A SWEET ONE— GOT PURTIER EVERY DAY—

MEBBE WARN'T SUCH A GOOD GAL ALLA TIME BUT CAIN'T BLAME 'ER—

ALL INNA BLOOD, Y' KNOW.

NAW, I WARN'T REALLY NO BLOOD KIN, BUT WHY TELL HER THAT?

ALL BE THE SAME INNA HUNDERD YEARS....

SHE'S A BITCH.

YEAH.

YEAH.

TALKING ABOUT M, RIGHT? SOME PEOPLE ARE SO AMAZING ALL THEY NEED IS ONE NAME, RIGHT? M'S ACTUALLY DOWN TO ONE LETTER.

SHE'S WASTED ON ONE LITTLE MILITARY MAN, NO MATTER HOW LOUD HE IS—

HELL, HER TITS ALONE COULD RUN THIS WORLD BETTER!

AS PREJUDICED AS ANY AGAINST THE CAUSE OF EQUAL RIGHTS FOR CONSTRUCTS.

WHAT'S THAT DUMB JOCK SKINJOB GOT THAT I HAVEN'T GOT?

LIPS.

FUCK YOU!

NO! NOT ALL THESE OTHER IDIOTS— SHOW ME EMMA!

I AM PSYCHOLOGICALLY DIVERGENT.

I SUFFER— IF THAT IS THE CORRECT TERM —FROM "PRINCESS" PSYCHOSIS.

WITHIN MY MIND IS A DOOR TO ANOTHER PLACE, GAN GARIDAN. IT IS FAR MORE REAL TO ME THAN THIS, THE BAD WORLD. IT HAS ITS OWN DEITIES, A DISCRETE AND SUBTLE LANGUAGE, GEOGRAPHY, AND PHYSICS, AND WITHIN IT, I AM QUEEN.

WHEN THE BAD WORLD PUSHES ME OUT, I GO HOME. I WALK IN SHINING FORESTS, I SPEAK IN GLORY. I JOIN THE SINGING THRONGS IN THE STONE STREETS.

AT SUCH TIMES, MY "MIRROR IMAGE" GOES ABOUT MY DAILY LIFE. IT SAYS NOTHING OF THIS— FOR IT CAN'T - AND NO ONE'S THE WISER.

BUT I MISS MY CHILDREN. I CAN'T TAKE THEM WITH ME TO MY HOME. I OFTEN WISH TO COME BACK AND CAN'T. AT THE WORST OF THE FEARS MY HUSBAND PUT ON ME, I LOST TWO YEARS OF MY BABIES' LIVES. I KNOW WHAT HAPPENED, BUT I FELT NONE OF IT...

MY DAUGHTER RACHEL IS MYSELF, YOUNG, BEFORE BRIGHAM.

SHE TELLS ME THAT THE DOOR TO EO OPENED BECAUSE OF BRIGHAM'S ABUSE.

HOW CAN I DOUBT HER?

THE ONLY REASON I AM FREE TO ROAM THE BAD WORLD AT WILL IS THE FACT THAT BRIG IS FAR FROM HERE. CONTAINED.

IT'S HARD TO PICTURE.

YOU WANT TO KNOW MY WORST FEAR?

HORAGOROSI. THAT'S MY END OF THE WORLD, MY RAGNAROK, FOR BRIGHAM TO GET OUT. THAT WOULD BE THE WORST THING.

HE WAS MY PLATOON LIEUTENANT WHILE I WAS IN THE BELLY OF THE BEAST.

HE GOT PROMOTED AWAY AND I HARDLY SAW HIM ANYMORE... BUT I'D STILL GO SEE M AND THE KIDS.

HE NEVER SEEMED TO BE THERE, EITHER....

THEN I GOT HURT AND WAS DISCHARGED— DIDN'T SEE ANY OF 'EM FOR AGES— EMMA POPS UP IN ANVARD WITH NO BRIGHAM— I'D GO SEE 'EM, BUT WHAT BUSINESS OF MINE WAS ALL OF THAT?

AND STILL I NEVER KNEW WHAT SHE'D BEEN THROUGH.

LIKE WITH MY FATHER. I FELT LIKE I WAS— KEEPING AN UNSPOKEN AGREEMENT—

HEYA, CHOAD SMOKER!

'JA BRING ME PICTURES OF MY LADIES?

OHH, YEAH—

THREE GIRLS, FOUR YEARS AND FOUR MONTHS APART EXACTLY. AN' THEIR MOM WAS THIRTY-FOUR WHEN WE GOT MARRIED.

HOWZAT FOR PRECISION, RECRUIT!

worst thing... worst...

HE'S HERE IN THIS CITY. AND EMMA DOESN'T KNOW. BUT HE KNOWS JUST WHERE THEY ARE.... ALWAYS HAS.... THANKS TO ME.

HE SAID.... SHE'D JUST UPPED AND LEFT HIM.... TOOK THE KIDS... SAID HE WANTED 'EM BACK... SAID HE... KNEW HOW ...TO WORK ON 'EM...

THANKS, BUDDY. I TRULY CAN'T THANK YOU ENOUGH.

SHOOOOOP!

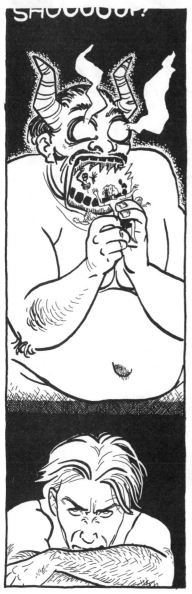

SHOOOOOP!

SHOOOOOP!

HOW COULD YOU?

SHOOOOOP!

MMY HHERO....

HHOW CAN I EVER RREPAYY YYOU?

67

SHOOOOP!

WELL. **NOW** WHAT?

I CAN'T FEEL WHERE THE DOOR IS.

THIS ROOM SWALLOWS UP SOUND AND SCENT.

IT COULD BE ANYWHERE OR NOWHERE.

THIS ROOM COULD BE ANY SHAPE AT ALL.

LET ME OUT!

PAYMENT IS DUE. IN FULL.

FUU--UCK.--

OKAY, OKAY.

THE THING I'M MOST AFRAID OF.

I HAVE A DISEASE.

AT LEAST THAT'S WHAT I THINK IT IS.

SEEMS LIKE, EVERY TIME I FIND A PLACE TO SETTLE, BACK IT COMES, ALL SMILEY.

AND IT GETS WORSE AND WORSE UNTIL I GET MOVING AND STIR SOME MORE SHIT UP.

IT NEVER GETS TO WHERE I FEEL LIKE I'LL DIE.

I JUST **WANT** TO.

IT DOESN'T MAKE SENSE ....

I CAN HANDLE **ANYTHING EXCEPT** PEACE AND QUIET?

AND I THINK, WHAT IF IT GETS WORSE? WHAT WILL I HAVE TO DO TO GET RID OF IT **NEXT** TIME?

WHRUMM

THANKS FOR THE SOUR PERSIMMONS, COUSIN.

SHOULD'VE KNOWN BETTER THAN TO GO TO THEM.

NO PARKING EVER EVER EVER

ANYTHING THEY TELL ME CAN'T HELP BUT BE WORST-CASE SCENARIOS.

AND THEY ALWAYS END UP TAKING MORE THAN THEY GIVE.

NO PARKING EVER EVER EVER

HEY, CAP. WE GOTTA SITUATION HERE.

LOVELY. WHAT?

WE WERE TURNING OUT ALL THE PICKUPS FROM THAT STREET PARTY — THIS ONE SAYS HIS CAR GOT TOWED FROM IN FRONT OF THE PAINWRIGHT GALLERY. NOW HE WANTS TO PAY UP AND TAKE IT.

YEAH — BUT ?

VRIIII... VRIIII... VRIII...

WELL, HIS STORY CHECKS OUT FINE, BUT HIS CAR DOESN'T. IT DID GET TICKET-AND-TOWED, IT DID GET CHECKED INTO THE LOT, BUT IT AIN'T THERE NOW.

SO WHERE IS IT?

..... NO CLUE.

COULD BE ONE OF THOSE TOW-TRUCK WEASELS BAGGED IT BACK OUT, AND IT'S IN A CHOP SHOP BY NOW. NICE CAR, LOTSA GOODIES.

SWELL.

JUST FAT SWELL.

WHAT ABOUT HIM ?

TYPICAL BROWNWAYS TYPE. NO RECORD, BUT NO I.D. EITHER, EXCEPT FOR LICENSE AND PROOF OF OWNERSHIP ON HIS BUGGY.

MAGNIFICATION 300

RUNAWAY

LOST

WANT

LIKE YOU COULD EVEN LOOK AT A CAR THAT HOT WITHOUT A PAPER TRAIL TEN MILES LONG!

SIGH ....

ALL RIGHT, I'VE GOT IT.

OKAY, MR. LENNOX. YOU GOT US. YOU'RE HERE, AND YOUR CAR'S NOT.

NOW THIS HAS HAPPENED A HUNDRED TIMES IN THE LAST SIX MONTHS, AND FRANKLY I DON'T FEEL LIKE GOING THROUGH THE WHOLE SCRIPT.

YOUR CAR'S NOT GOING TO TURN UP. AT LEAST NOT INTACT.

I SUPPOSE YOU GOTTA HAVE CASH, RIGHT? NO BANK ACCOUNT OR CREDIT I.D., RIGHT?

RIGHT.

HERE.

DON'T MAKE THIS WORSE BY COUNTING IT.

I SUPPOSE THIS MIGHT BE MISINTERPRETED AS A CHARITABLE ACT. TAKES NO GREAT BRAIN TO SEE THAT THE FIRST FAMILIES' WAYS MAKE IT HARD FOR YOU MIXED-BLOOD BROWNWAYS TYPES TO MAKE A DECENT LIVING. BUT I'D JUST AS SOON NOT HAVE MY NOSE RUBBED IN IT.

UNDERSTAND?

YOU'RE A CYNICAL MAN, CAPTAIN ASIAK.

AND YOU'RE A TWO-BIT SCAM ARTIST. GET OUTTA HERE AND STAY OUT OF MY SIGHT.

PETE? SURE, I GOT IT.

OH, AND THANKS **SO MUCH** FOR SENDING ME OUT ON A JOB SO STALE THE COPS KNOW ALL ABOUT IT.

I DON'T **GIVE** TWO FARTS IN A HURRICANE THAT THEY CAN'T DO ANYTHING TO ME.

I DON'T **EE**-VEN CARE WHAT YOU HAD TO DO TO GET JERRY LOCKWOOD'S TOWING COMPANY IN ON THIS.

I **AIN'T** RUNNING YOUR ERRANDS JUST TO BE A **TARGET** FOR THE TIN-TEDDIES TO **VENT** ON!

WHAT-? WHAT **ABOUT** LEMONS?

WHA' TH' **FUCK** ARE YOU **TAKING**, YOU GOAT RAPER??

SHIT!

K'KLANGG!

AT **LEAST** IN THE WOODS ALL THE PREDATORS ARE AFTER IS YOUR BODY, NOT YOUR SANITY!

THE FINDERS ARE NOW MAINLY FORGOTTEN.

THEY WERE HUNTERS, AND TRACKERS, AND MORE.

THEY LIVED SECRET LIVES.

MOST PEOPLE DIDN'T KNOW WHO HAD OR HADN'T BEEN ACCEPTED INTO THEIR SECRET SOCIETY.

THEIR SKILLS WERE HONED TO ARTISTRY.

TO CATCH THE SLIGHTEST GLIMPSE OF ONE AGAINST HIS INTENT WAS RARE INDEED, AND BROUGHT GREAT CENSURE FROM HIS BRETHREN.

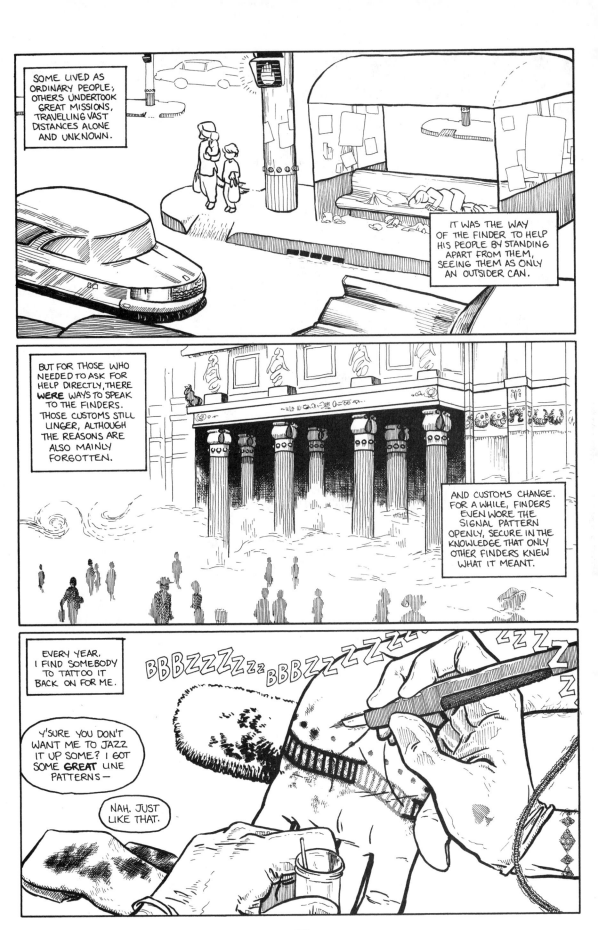

SOME LIVED AS ORDINARY PEOPLE; OTHERS UNDERTOOK GREAT MISSIONS, TRAVELLING VAST DISTANCES ALONE AND UNKNOWN.

IT WAS THE WAY OF THE FINDER TO HELP HIS PEOPLE BY STANDING APART FROM THEM, SEEING THEM AS ONLY AN OUTSIDER CAN.

BUT FOR THOSE WHO NEEDED TO ASK FOR HELP DIRECTLY, THERE **WERE** WAYS TO SPEAK TO THE FINDERS. THOSE CUSTOMS STILL LINGER, ALTHOUGH THE REASONS ARE ALSO MAINLY FORGOTTEN.

AND CUSTOMS CHANGE. FOR A WHILE, FINDERS EVEN WORE THE SIGNAL PATTERN OPENLY, SECURE IN THE KNOWLEDGE THAT ONLY OTHER FINDERS KNEW WHAT IT MEANT.

EVERY YEAR, I FIND SOMEBODY TO TATTOO IT BACK ON FOR ME.

BBBZZZZZz BBBZZZZZZZZZZ ZZZ

Y'SURE YOU DON'T WANT ME TO JAZZ IT UP SOME? I GOT SOME **GREAT** LINE PATTERNS—

NAH. JUST LIKE THAT.

IN CITIES, I NEED ALL THE HELP I CAN GET TO REMEMBER WHO I AM.
KTOKk
<SOFT LANDING>

HELLO, BRIGHAM.

HOW'S THE WIFE AND KIDS?

YOU TELL ME, MAN.

AIN'T THAT WHAT I PAY YOU THE BIG BUCKS TO FIND OUT?

SO? GIVE!

OHH, YEAH.

HI, BABY.

OH, GOD. IT'S SO GOOD TO SEE YOU.

MY BEAUTIFUL BABIES.

77

TAKTAKKATAKKA TAKATAK TAK TAK TAKKAKATAKA .. TAK .. TAK TAKKATA.. TAKTAK

TAKTAK TAK TAKKAKATAKA TAKKATAK TIK TIK TAKKATA TAKTK TAK TAKKA TAK TAKTIK TAKKA TAK TAKTAKKA

LYNNE!

WHY CAN'T YOU **LEAVE** HER **ALONE**?

SHE **MIGHT** JUST GET **WELL** IF YOU **DID**, YOU KNOW!

THAT REGULATOR **IS A DOCTOR'S TOOL!**

I **KNOW** BEING A **GENIUS** GIVES YOU THE **DIVINE RIGHT** TO SCREW AROUND WITH ANYTHING YOU CAN GET YOUR HANDS ON, BUT DON'T YOU **EVER** STOP TO WONDER IF YOU **SHOULD**??

AND **PUT** THAT **THING OUT!**

THIS **IS** ONE OF HER **FAVORITE** DRESSES, YOU KNOW!

IF YOU **REALLY** CARED ABOUT HER, YOU'D CARE ABOUT WHAT **SHE** WANTS!

IF YOU'RE **THAT** CONCERNED ABOUT THE STATE OF HER CLOTHES, **MAYBE** YOU SHOULD DO **YOUR** SHARE OF THE LAUNDRY, LITTLE MISS IF-I-DON'T-DO -IT-IT-WON'T-GET-DONE.

I MIGHT AS WELL BE WHISTLING THROUGH MY NOSE AS TALKING TO YOU ANYMORE.

≡COFF≡

GIRRRL.

```
> OPEN CONNECTION
# IMD PROTOCOL ENABLED
.... CONNECTION ESTABLISHED
$ CHKCONFIG DIAGMODE ON
OK
$ CHKCONFIG DEBUG ON
OK
$ CAT /dev /kmem >/dev /console
QXX!#@A⊖^ ♪4;ZΩΨO♂ ⊕
Rr Rr Rr ⊙ 9⅃ HD♀÷/÷♭T∞$B
```

```
8i~⊞ᖶ☆∅........
# whoami
root

# OPEN INTERFACE 2: MARCIE
DOCTOR TO PATIENT CONNECTION
...... ESTABLISHED

#_
```

DOWNLOAD FILES

NNN!

▷ DON'T WORRY, MARS.

▷ IF DEAR OLD DAD **DOES** COME BACK, YOU'LL BE READY.

BRIGHAM.... ALL THIS TIME YOU'VE BEEN IN STIR, I BEEN LOOKIN' IN ON YOUR FAMILY FOR YOU.

HAVE THEY **EVER** SO MUCH AS SENT YA A **TIE** ON **FATHER'S DAY?** A **PHONE** CALL? A GANG RAPE GET-WELL CARD? **ANY**THING?

WHAT'S IT TO **YOU?**

THOUGHT NOT. WHY **DID** EMMA LEAVE YOU?

WHAT'S SHE BEEN TELLING YOU?

WHATEVER IT IS, IT AIN'T THE WHOLE STORY.

FINE. SO?

DAMMIT, YOU'VE GOT **NO** RIGHT TO GET BETWEEN ME AND MY **FAMILY!** THIS IS **NONE** OF YOUR **BUSINESS!!**

NONE OF MY BUSINESS?? JEEZUS, BRIGHAM!

THREE YEARS YOU'VE BEEN BEGGIN' ME— "C'MON, C'MON, JUST CHECK UP ON 'EM~ SO I'LL KNOW THEY'RE OKAY, CAUSE I'M SO ALOOOONE, DO IT FOR MEEEE, MAN!" SHIT!

81

IT'S PART OF THE **DEAL** FOR OFFICERS — WHY ELSE D'YOU THINK I **WANTED** A COMMISSION?

THAT'S WHAT THE FREE TRADERS' PACT IS FOR — **NOT** JUST SO THOSE DAMN INDIANS AND GYPSIES AND SHIT YOU LOVE SO MUCH CAN BUY AND SELL WITHOUT CITIZENSHIPS!

I **FINALLY** GOT SENT INTO A BATTLEZONE WORTH **SETTLING** WITH ENOUGH RANK TO **DO** IT, SO I **DID!**

LAND FOR PEACE!

AIN'T NOTHING **ILLEGAL** <u>ABOUT</u> IT!

NO, NOT TO **YOU**.

SO **HOW** COME EMMA DIDN'T KNOW ABOUT THIS?

—NO, SHE DIDN'T.

YEAH... WELL, THAT'S EMMA.

SHE PUTS UP A GOOD FRONT, BUT SHE'S **NOT** OKAY. HOW CAN YOU TELL HER **EVERY- THING** IF YOU NEVER KNOW WHAT'LL SET HER OFF?

YOU END UP TELLING HER **NOTHING**.

YEAH ....

YEAH, I GUESS I **DID** KNOW THAT.

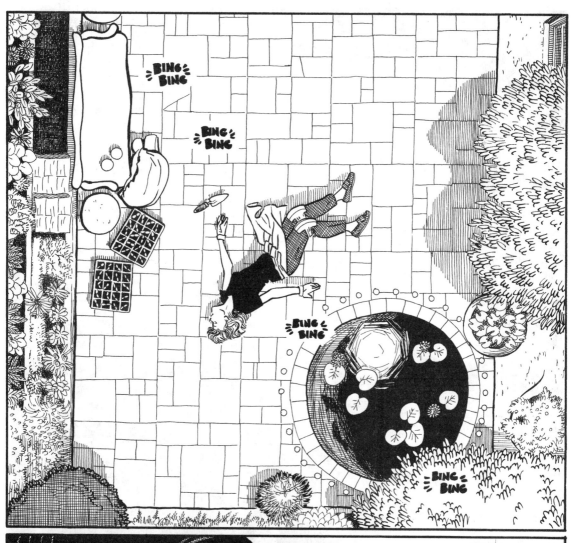

(THIS GUY) THE SKY

HAS

TWO MOONS

AND

ONE SON

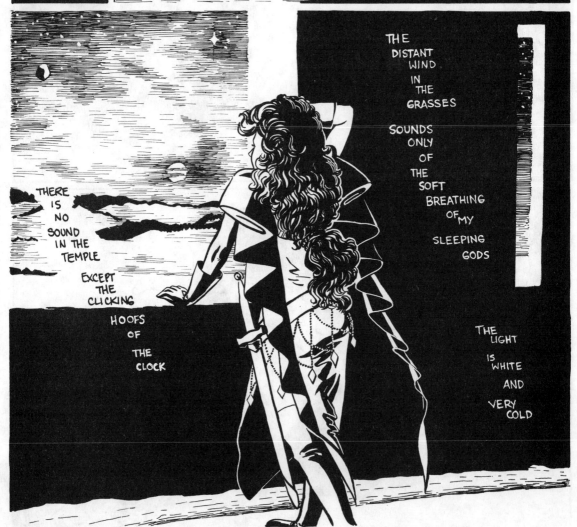

THE DISTANT WIND IN THE GRASSES

SOUNDS ONLY OF THE SOFT BREATHING OF MY SLEEPING GODS

THERE IS NO SOUND IN THE TEMPLE

EXCEPT THE CLICKING

HOOFS OF THE CLOCK

THE LIGHT IS WHITE AND VERY COLD

REMIND ME, WON'T YOU, BLYTHE? I'M JUST.. HAVING ONE OF MY DAYS...

BIEN SUR, MADAME. DOES MADAME WEESH ZAT ALL 'ER CALLS BE 'ELD TODAY?

JUST CAN'T SEEM TO GET IT TOGETHER...

MADAME~ oOOT!?

EH... PAUVRE MADAME EMMA! STRAHNJ' DAYS, INDEED!

EH?

♪ ...I LEFT A NOTE ... ...ON HIS DRESSER... ...WITH MY OLD... ♪ ...WEDDING RING....

PING!

BLYTHE! BAD PROGRAM! NEVER LISTEN IN UNINVITED!

♪ ...WITH THESE FEW.. GOODBYE WORDS... ...HOW CAN... I SING...? ...GOODBYE, OLD SLEEPYHEAD... ♪ ...I'M PACKIN' YOU IN... ♪ TAKE CARE... ...OF EVERYTHING...

BUTT OUT! THIS COULD BE IMPORTANT!

YEAH, YEAH, BUT MADAME'S THERAPY!!

BUT MADAME'S PRIVACY~

PING!

(HUMMING EDITH PIAF)

♪ ...I'M LEAVING MY WEDDING RING... ...DON'T LOOK FOR ME ..... ♪

♪ ...I'LL GET AHEAD.... ...REMEMBER, DARLING... ...DON'T SMOKE.... ♪ ... IN BED....

STHENO

TIKATIKATIKTIK TIKKATIK TIK TIK TIK TIKKA TIK

SO... WHAT ABOUT THE GIRLS?

WHAT ABOUT 'EM?

IF EMMA'S GONE CRACKERS, HOW DO YOU KNOW **THEY** HAVEN'T **TOO?** THEY WENT THROUGH THE SAME—

THEY AIN'T **NOTHING** WRONG WITH MY KIDS. RACHEL MAY **LOOK** LIKE EMMA'S CLAN, BUT SHE'S MEDAWAR TO THE BONE. SHE'LL FIGURE **THAT** OUT SOON ENOUGH.

HEY HO   WHO IS THERE
NO ONE BUT ME MY DEAR
   PLEASE COME   SAY HOW DO
THE THINGS I'LL GIVE TO YOU
A STROKE AS GENTLE
      AS A FEATHER

   HEY HO   I AM HERE
AM I NOT YOUNG AND FAIR
PLEEASE COME
         SAY HOW DO
WOULD YOU HAVE
      A WONDROUS SIGHT?
MIDDAY SUN
         AT MIDNIGHT

   FAIR MAID
         WHITE AND RED
   COMB YOU SMOOTH
         AND STROKE YOUR HEAD

CHUG CHUG CHUG CHUG

=SIGH=

LINT

WE! CARRY! DEATH! OUT! OF THE VILLAGE!

WE! CARRY! DEATH! OUT! OF THE VILLAGE!

WE! CARRY! DEATH! OUT! OF THE VILLAGE!

WE! CARRY! DEATH! OUT! OF THE VILLAGE!

WE! CARRY! DEATH! OUT! OF THE VILLAGE!

WE! CARRY! DEATH! OUT! OF THE VILLAGE!

WE! CARRY! DEATH! OUT! OF THE VILLAGE!

=TSK=

THEY COULD AT **LEAST** MAKE HER WALK AT THE BITTER END.

BRIG JUST **NEVER** SHOULDA MARRIED THAT LLAVERAC WOMAN. IT'S THE END FOR HIS CAREER.

NOW, NOW... RACHEL'S A VERY SWEET AND RESPECT- FUL GIRL.

-PEG-

—**AND** HER MOTHER'S THE BEST BOTANIST WE'VE EVER HAD.

THEY PULL THEIR WEIGHT, SO SAVE THE CLAN SNOBBERY.

BESIDES, SHE'S JUST A KID, AND IT'S SPRING FESTIVAL, SO **DON'T** YOU TWO BUMS SPOIL EVERYBODY'S FUN. WORRY ABOUT RACHEL WHEN SHE'S OLD ENOUGH TO BE **TROUBLE.**

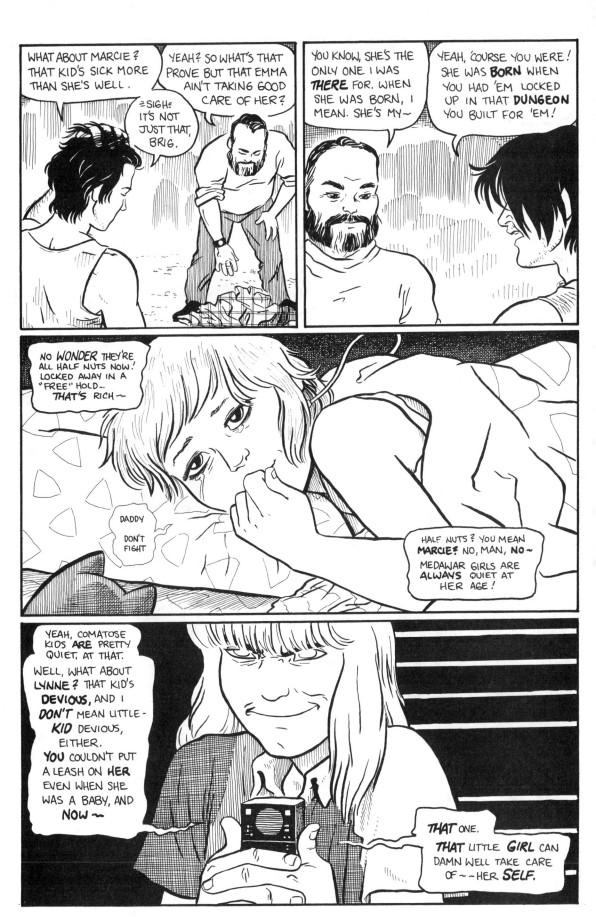

BRIG, SHE'S **TEN**! YOU DON'T TOSS A TEN-YEAR-OLD OUT TO FEND FOR HERSELF—

OH, NO? HOW OLD WERE **YOU** WHEN YOU LEFT **YOUR** FATHER'S HOUSE?

JAEGER, YOU DON'T **REALLY** WANT TO **STAY** IN THE MIDDLE OF THIS, DO YA?

NOT REALLY YOUR **STYLE**.

WHERE THEY AT?

MY SOUNDTRACK MUSTA BEEN WORKING OVERTIME, 'CAUSE ALL I COULD THINK OF WAS A LINE FROM A SONG I'D HEARD A MILLION TIMES A DAY DURING MY STINT IN THE ARMY:

"IF YA WANNA FIND OUT WHAT'S BEHIND THESE COLD EYES Y'LL JUST HAF TA CLAW YER WAY THROUGH THIS DISGUISE"

(....HATE THAT SONG...)

WOULD HE FLIP OUT AND ATTACK ME IF I SAID NO?

SHOULD I JUST PSS HIM OFF AND **MAKE** HIM TRY FOR ME?

(GET IT OVER WITH)

HIS PULSE IS HIGH, HIS PUPILS BIG AS EGGS.

HE'S AFRAID. HE'S ANGRY.

WHAT **ELSE** IS HE?

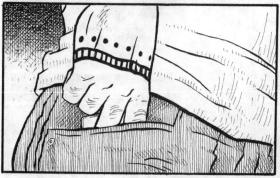

93

I CLEANED THAT POOR OL' FART UP AND GAVE 'IM TWELVE BUCKS AND JUST LIKE THAT WE'RE BUDDY PALS.

BUT **I** STILL FELT LIKE A TOTAL **BONEHEAD** AND I HAD TO DO **SOMETHING** TO AVOID GOING INTO A FUNK.

DISPOSABLE SOCIETY, LTD. CATHARTIC KICK-STARTS WHITE ELEPHANTS EXTERMINATED PSYCHOLOGICAL BAGGAGE LOST

THANKS, MAN. YOU GOTTA **GREAT** THING GOING HERE!

HEAR ye, **HEAR** ye! PEOPLE of **ANVARD,** ye are **SLAVES!**

SLAVES, yes, **SLAVES** to "**NEW** AND **IMPROVED**" and "**HIGHER UPGRADE**"! **WET**ware, **HARD**ware, **SOFT**ware!

HOW MANY **TIMES** HAVE YOU **SCRAPED** and **SAVED** and **GONE WITHOUT** FOR SOMETHING YOU **REALLY** couldn't **AFFORD?**

didja **LOSE SLEEP** WISHIN' YOU **HAD** it? **QUESTION** the VERY **FABRIC** OF YOUR **EXISTENCE** because **YOU DON'T MAKE** ENOUGH to **HAVE** it **RIGHT NOW?**

99

WELL, IT'S **JUST** LIKE THIS CONCENTRATION ENHANCER I BOUGHT **LAST** YEAR-- IT'S **TOP** OF THE **LINE**, BUT THE **EX**TRA FEATURES SCREW UP THE **STAN**DARD ONES!

WELL **DAMN**.

AND IT'S GOT AN EVEN **SHORTER** WARRANTY THAN THE **LAST** ONE DID AND I JUST CAN'T **FACE** WARRANTY COURT AGAIN..

IT COST SO **MUCH**... I JUST WANTED TO, YOU KNOW, **TREAT** MYSELF...

AWWWW TSK-TSK-TSK.

IT'S **JUST** SO **FRUS**TRATING! YOU **SPEND** SO MUCH, IT **OUGHT** TO **WORK** RIGHT!

DIDJA EVEN **TRY** TO GET THE SHOP TO TAKE IT BACK?

HUH (?)

OH ~ UH ~ IT'S SO EMBARRAS - I ~

NEVER MIND-

SISTAH, THE WAR-CRY "**LET'S GO SHOPPING**" IS THE CALL OF THE **DOOMED**! **STEP** RIGHT UP AND **FIND** THE **ANSWER**!

≡GRUNT≡

whimper ~

RE**MEM**BER, SIS, THE HARDEST CHAINS TO BREAK ARE THE VELVET ONES.

SCR//'//EE

BRSZZZZ

HELLO ♪! I AM YOUR PERSONALIZABLE ARTIFICIAL INTELLI-GENCE - PLEASE SUBMIT THE FOLLOWING PERSONAL INFORMA-TION TO OBTAIN YOUR PASSWORD!

OTHER WISE, YOU'RE STUCK WITH ME! ≡hee hee hee≡ EEEEK!

FREEP!

BLANG!

DIE FUCKER! DIE FUCKER! DIE

E___WATER FASHIO___

I JUST NEVER COULD'VE TAKEN THAT FIRST SWING!

NOT A PROBLEM, THAT'S WHAT I'M HERE FOR.

JUST PISSIN' IN THE OCEAN, MAN.

I'M FREE, FREE! I CAN BUY A GOOD ONE NOW!

WELL, I GUESS THAT OCEAN HAD TO COME FROM SOMEWHERE.

HEY, PETE. JAEGER. I GOTTA 'NOTHER LOAD FOR YA.

YEAH, YOU'RE FUNNY. WHATTA YOU DO WITH ALL THIS BUSTED-UP ELECTRONIC CRAP?

YEAHYEAH. QUICK MIKE MELTS IT DOWN. THAR'S GOLD ON THEM THAR CIRCUIT BOARDS, YA IGNRINT HICK. CRYSTALS IN THE POWER SUPPLY TOO.

SHIT, YOU BELIEVE IN RECYCLING, DON'TCHA?

YEAHYEAH, SURE YA DO. THOSE FOLKS KNOW THAT SHIT'S THERE, THEY'RE JUST LAZY. WE'S JUST AVAILIN' OURSELVES OF GOOD OPPORTUNITY.

CORNER OF FIFTH AND ROYLE? SURE THING, YEAHYEAH.

ONLY HE COULD PULL OFF A SCAM LIKE THAT ONE. IT'S RIDICULOUS.

S'CUZ HE REALLY B'LIEVES THAT ANTI-COMMERCIAL CRAPOLA.

SO, HE'S KINDA CRACKERS. ALL THEM TREE-HANGERS ARE. HE'S A GOOD EARNER. =HURRGRETCH=

SONNY SITS BY HIS WINDOW AND THINKS TO HIMSELF

HOW IT'S STRANGE THAT SOME ROOMS ARE LIKE CAGES

SONNY'S YEARBOOK FROM HIGH SCHOOL IS DOWN FROM THE SHELF AND HE IDLY THUMBS THROUGH THE PAGES SOME HAVE DIED SOME HAVE FLED FROM THEMSELVES OR STRUGGLED FROM HERE TO GET THERE

SONNY WANDERS BEYOND HIS INTERIOR WALLS RUNS HIS HANDS THROUGH HIS THINNING BROWN HAIR WELL I'M ACC RRRIP AND THAT'S ENOUGHA THAT! WELCOME TO ECLECTIC RADIO, WHERE WE NEVER WAIT TILL THE SONG'S OVER TO START TALKING!

THAT WAS SOMETHING-OR-OTHER BY SOME DEAD SOMEBODY WHO WAS JUST REMEMBERED BY THOSE FINE FINE PEOPLE AT THE PASTWATCH INSTITUTE FOR ALL YOU EVERYBODIES WHO CLING DESPERATELY TO THE CULTURE OF THE PAST RATHER THAN DISTILL ANYTHING NEW OUT OF THE PRESENT.

MMWAH!

THE INSTITUTE HAS ALSO RECENTLY REINTRODUCED THESE BLASTS FROM THE PAST: FREEZE-DRIED ICE CREAM, WINE IN A BOX, COCAINE IN GREEN GLASS BOTTLES, AND PAINFUL CORSETRY.

BOY- OH, WEREN'T THE PEOPLE OF THE ANCIENT WORLD GENIUSES. HOP ON DOWN TO THE CORNER STORE AND CONSUME, CONSUME, CONSUME!

WOW, WHAT A BORING SUMMER. WE HAVEN'T EVEN TURNED UP A GOOD SERIAL KILLER. C'MON, GUYS, 'RE OUT HERE, WE LOOK LIKE YOUR MOTHERS, AND WE STILL THINK YOU'RE LOSERS.

WELL, TEN SECONDS TO KILL, HO HO HO; DOES ANYBODY REMEMBER "CONJUNCTION JUNCTION"? NO? TOO BAD....

WE NOW RETURN TO OUR SEGMENT ON LIFE IN THE MILITARY! TODAY WE'RE TAKING A LOOK AT RELIGION! IT'S WELL-KNOWN THAT THE REALITIES OF LIVING IN FEAR FOR ONE'S LIFE=

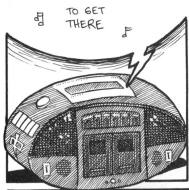

IS **DAT** FOR **MEE?**

NO SIR IT'S FOR YOUR **DAUGHTER** SIR!

KEEP **GOIN'**, IRON MAN! EIGHTY-**SIX!** EIGHTY-**SEVEN!** EIGHTY-**EIGHT!**

THANK YOU **GOD!** THANK YOU **GOD!** THANK YOU **GOD!**

WHIZZ

GYAAH!

IS **DAT** FOR **MEE?**

=GASPP= -SHIT- =WHEEZ= -FUCK-

GOD **DAMMIT**, JAEGER!

HOW DO YOU **DO** THAT SHIT??

IT AIN'T SO TOUGH TO LEARN IF YOU PUT YOUR MIND TO IT.

WELL, C'MON, WEASEL. PITCH IN. THIS OL' GAL'S FAMILY'LL BE BACK TOMORROW.

UHH HUH. SIT IN YOUR **OWN** WET SPOT, BRIGHAM.

ALL RIGHT.

LYING IS LIKE ALCOHOLISM.

RECOVERING FROM IT IS A LIFETIME THING. YOU EITHER DIE **DOING** IT OR TRYING **NOT** TO DO IT.

BAJARE FAMILY

NOT HARD TO TELL BRIGHAM'S FALLEN OFF THE WAGON. NOT TO ME, ANYWAY.

THE QUESTION IS NOT **WHETHER** HE'LL LIE TO ME BUT HOW **WELL** HE'LL LIE.

SNF

AHH— DAMN!

SO— WHAT AM **I** DOING HERE?

ENGAGING IN A WEIRD FETISH.

SWUTCHA SWUTCHA

JERKASS!

THIS IS SORTA MY DAY JOB. PAYS WELL, BUT IT'S SPORADIC.

SMAK!

LOCAL COPS ARE MEDAWARS. THEY MAY BE PIGS, BUT THEY'RE FAMILY.

SEE, COPS JUST RUN DOWN CRIME SCENES. WHAT HAPPENS AFTER? THE FAMILY HAS TO SCRUB THEIR BLOOD KIN OFF THE CEILING. FIGURE OUT HOW TO GET IT OUT OF THE SOFA. **BAD**, BAD NEWS. PEOPLE DOING THIS KIND OF CLEANUP WORK SPARES THE FAMILY SOME PAIN.

...YEAH.

SOP!

SO....
WHATCHA DOIN' FOR MONEY THESE DAYS?

FINDER'S FEES... PROB'LY GET SOME WORK FROM THE ARCHAEOLOGY COLLEGE WHEN DIG SEASON BEGINS.

NO, MAN, I MEAN A J.O.B., **YOU** KNOW, CONTRIBUTING MEMBER OF SOCIETY KIND OF THING?

AHH, BRIG, WHATYA **DO**, GET YER SOCIAL WORKER'S LICENSE IN THE PRISON REHAB PROGRAM?

≡KEE-REIST!≡ YOU **PISS** ME OFF, YOU **KNOW** THAT??

EVERYBODY TELLS ME, DO WHAT YOU LOVE, THE MONEY WILL FOLLOW.

WELL, SOMEDAY SOON **YOU'RE** GONNA BE SOME **KINDA** RICH FUCKER!

BUT JAEGER— **SHIT!** YOU GOT EVERYTHING YOU **NEED** TO MAKE IT. TO BE AN **EXAMPLE.** TO BETTER YOUR **KIND!**

MY KIND.

WELL **GOD DAMMIT, SO** YOU WEREN'T BORN INTO A CLAN! SO DAMN MANY OF YOU MIXED-BLOODS JUST **GIVE UP!** JUST **DRIFT** THROUGH LIFE!

YOU GOT BRAINS, LOOKS, **SPINE,** AND YOU'RE JUST GONNA BE A **SCAVENGER** ALL YOUR LIFE? COME **ON,** KID!

STICK WITH **ME,** JAEGER.

I'LL GET YOU HONEST WORK.

I NOTICED ALSO THAT THIS LADY'S NAME WAS EMMA.

HUH?

NAW. DAVIS. HELLENA DAVIS. BAJARE CLAN.

HELLENA'S HER **SECOND** NAME. **EMMA** HELLENA DAVIS.

WELL—

—IT'S A COMMON ENOUGH NAME.

EMMA HELLENA DAVIS

WEYLL— GLAD OF THE HELP, BUD. YOU THINK ABOUT WHAT I SAID.

I IMAGINE **YOU** CAN FIND YOUR **OWN** WAY **OUT,** HUH?

I GOT TO GET MOVIN'—THINGS TO GO, PEOPLE TO DO.

SO YOU HAVE, BRIG.

SO YOU HAVE.

LLAVERAC CLAN HOME HIGH SCHOOL

WRIIIINNNGGG!

FUCK YOU
FUCK YOU
FUCK YOU
FUCK YOU

SNICKER

GIGGLE

TSK-TSK-TSK...
NICE MEN DON'T
HANG AROUND
SCHOOL YARDS.

~SSCRITTTCH

I'M JUST
PICKING UP MY
SIS ~ MY SISTER'S
KID.

UH
HUH.

WOOYAH... GOOD THING THEY
DON'T ALL **SMELL** ALIKE.

JAEGER!

MMFF ~~~

MMM~POP!

HELL, BABY,
DON'T STOP
NOW!

SO NICE
TO SEE AN
UNFAMILIAR
FACE!

111

HUH?

I DID IT. IT WAS ME.

YOU KICKED OUR DOOR DOWN??

YEAH, SO IT'S **OKAY**, OKAY?

IT'S **NOT** OKAY! **WHY** DID YOU **DO** IT??

I HAD TO GET **IN**, WHY ELSE?

WHAT WAS IN HERE THAT WAS **SO IMPORTANT** YOU **COULDN'T WAIT!?**

WHAT DIFFERENCE DOES IT MAKE?

WHAT **DIFF**-- **WHAT** DOES **THAT** MEAN??

IF YOU **DON'T** MIND MY BEING IN HERE WHEN YOU **ARE** HOME, **WHY** SHOULD YOU CARE IF I'M IN HERE WHEN YOU'RE **NOT?**

THAT'S RI DIC-- AAGH! **JUST** BECAUSE WE **TRUST** YOU ENOUGH TO --TO--TO-- **THAT DOESN'T** GIVE YOU THE RIGHT TO **BUST** THE PLACE **UP!**

DOOR WAS LOCKED, I NEEDED TO GET IN. REAL SIMPLE.

IT'S **NOT** SIMPLE!

LOOK. I'M **FIXIN'** IT, AIN'T I? IT WAS A CHEAP SHITTY DOORFRAME, I GOT YA A **GOOD** ONE. **NOT** THAT IT MATTERS MUCH **NOW.**

WHAT ARE YOU **TALKING** ABOUT?? AND **WHAT** ABOUT MY **MOM** AND MY **SISTERS?**

I DUNNO, GO **ASK** 'EM.

HUH?

HI SWEETIE, GO GET CHANGED! BUSY, BUSY, BUSY!

STUFF

MOM, DID YOU **KNOW** HE KICKED THE **DOOR** DOWN?

HEH! YES - LOST MY KEYS SOMEWHERE - DUMB LUCK, THAT -

YOU **ASKED** HIM TO DO IT?

NOOOO ~ BUT IT WAS **EFFECTIVE**, WASN'T IT?

AND THIS DOESN'T **BOTHER** YOU?

OHH, BABY, TODAY **NOTHING** BOTHERS ME!

LADIES AND GENTLEMEN, TODAY **NOTHING** BOTHERS EMMA GROSVENOR. SO WHAT'S THE **STORY?**

WE **GOT** THE GRASS HOUSE!

REALLY?!?

YES!

OHH, FOURTEEN **MONTHS** ON THE WAITING LIST, **ENDLESS** FIGHTS WITH THE AGENTS, **ALL** THAT **MONEY.** BUT MY DREAM HOUSE IS **MINE!!**

LIKE **MAGIC,** THEY CALLED, AND THE DEAL'S ALL SET!

VRRRR!

SO GO GET CHANGED, BABY. WE GOTTA GET OUTTA THIS MOUSEHOLE **NOW!** THE LEASE IS UP IN **TWO** DAYS, THANK **GOODNESS** I DI CLCN IT EARLY ~

CRINNKK

CREAK -SNAP-!

CLANK

CRINK!

CREEINK

DAMMIT, YOU BITCH! COME OUT OF THERE! YER COMIN' OUT IF I GOTTA SNAP YOU IN HALF!

CSM JULY 97

THERE IS NO SKY IN ANVARD.

ONE LOOKS UP AT BUILDINGS COLLAGED TOGETHER, GABLED AND BUTTRESSED AND GROWN INTO ONE ANOTHER LIKE SUGAR CRYSTALS.

NO STARS. NO MOON, NO WIND OR MISTS OR SNOW.

WHAT THERE IS ~ ARE ~ ARE ROOMS. ROOMS WITHIN ROOMS LIKE A HOLY CAVERN. FROM THE VAULTED CATHEDRAL HALLS OF THE GREAT HIGHWAYS TO THE VAST ARENAS DECORATED WITH STALAGMITES AND STALACTITES MADE NOT OF STONE BUT OF CONCRETE AND BRICK, STEEL AND GLASS.

LOOK DOWN AND YOU SEE BOTTOMLESS PITS. THE CITY DESCENDS FAR BELOW THE SURFACE OF THE LAND IT SITS ON.

WINDOWS SPARKLE IN THE GLOOM OF THE SUN-GLOBES.

IT'S A SUNLIGHT THAT NEVER MOVES WITH THE HOURS OR THE SEASONS. NEVER BRIGHT OR DARK.

NO RAIN CLEANS OUT THE DUSTY CORNERS.

ALL THE TREES IN POTS AND CAREFULLY TENDED GARDENS.

NETWORKS OF OPEN AQUEDUCTS SUFFICE FOR SUBTERRANEAN RIVERS, FEEDING LAKES AND POOLS ON EVERY LEVEL.

THE BURIAL CANOES OF THE CIMARGUE INDIANS PASS THROUGH ALL THIS CHAOS LARGELY UNTROUBLED, BORNE UP BY THE POISONOUS RED RIVER.

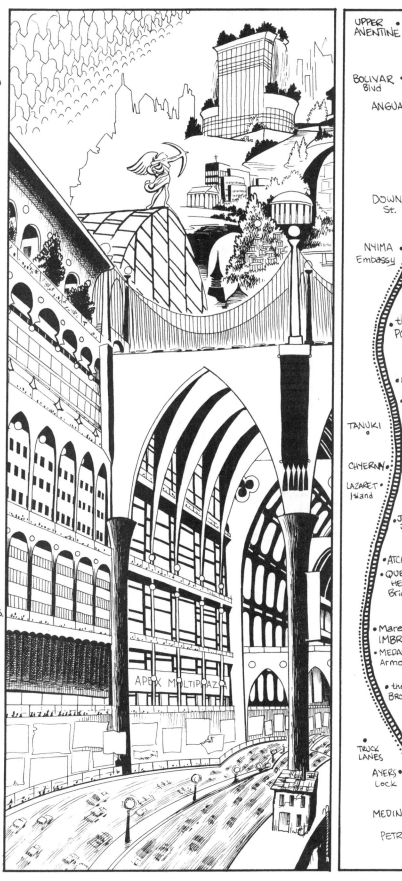

APEX MULTIPLAZA

UPPER AVENTINE
BOLIVAR Blvd
ANGUA
DOWNING St.
NYIMA Embassy
the POD
RISING Rd.
GULLA-HINGLA
TANUKI
CHYERNA
LAZARET Island
JORAN-JADRAN
ATCHAFALAYA
QUEENS' HEAD Bridge
Mare IMBRIUM
MEDAWAR Armory
the BROWNWAYS
TRUCK LANES
AYERS Lock
MEDINA
PETRUS

WE'RE TALKING THIS HOUR TO JOHN F. BOWLEGGED KENNEDY, DIRECTOR OF THE LONG-AWAITED FILM ADAPTATION OF THE NOVEL "THE KILLER INSIDE ME", LAUDED AS THE FINEST PERSPECTIVE NOVEL YET RECOVERED!

HEL LO EVERYBODY, IT'S THIRTEEN O'CLOCK; LUNCHTIME FOR DAYLIGHTERS, DREAMTIME FOR MIDNIGHTERS, AND WAKE-UP CALL FOR TWI-LIGHTERS! THIS IS CHANNEL 6XTC, SIX EXTASIES CITY BROADCASTING!

I CHOSE TO RENDER THIS FILM AS A STRAIGHT READING OF THE BOOK ILLUSTRATED BY STOCK FOOTAGE OF MURDERS AND WELL, SO ON TO PROVE A POINT. I MEAN, THIS NOVEL WAS WRITTEN IN ANTIQUITY, WHEN WE HAD VIRTUALLY NO UNDERSTANDING OF THE ROLE OF THE KILLER IN HUMAN SOCIETY, AND YET IT'S SO VIVIDLY REAL. THE WORK OF AN AUTHOR LIKE THAT OUGHT NOT TO BE TRIVIALIZED BY VISUAL STYLIZATION.

ul. SELACHIIE

HOT FAKE & DEAD

ALSO— THERE WAS NO REAL WAY TO BE TRUE TO THE FIRST-PERSON NARRATIVE SO VITAL TO THE INTENSE IDEN-TIFICATION WITH THE CHARACTER OF LOU FORD WITHOUT THE CONTINUOUS VOICE-OVER. YOU NEVER SEE LOU FORD'S FACE EXCEPT IN MIRRORS —

THE FILM WAS ASSEMBLED ALMOST ENTIRELY FROM STOCK FOOTAGE AND I DEFY ANYBODY TO CALL IT ANYTHING BUT SEAMLESS. EVERY SCENE IN THE BOOK WAS THERE TO BE FOUND, PLAYED OUT IN REAL LIFE, PRECISE AS RITUAL.

IT'S NICE, LIVING IN A CITY.

"THE KILLER INSIDE ME" WILL PREMIERE **RIGHT** HERE IN JUST **SEVEN** HOURS ~ AND WILL REPLAY FOR ALL THREE LIFECYCLES ~ IN OTHER ENTERTAINMENT NEWS, BLAH **BLAH** WAH **WAHH** WA WAHH **WAHHH** ~

NO **RAIN**, NO **SNOW**, NO COLD **WIND**, NO HOT SUMMER. NO THREE DIFFERENT WARDROBES TO KEEP UP WITH. AIR SCRUBBERS ON EVERY CORNER, AND ALL THE SUN YOU WANT FROM THE STREETLAMPS.

BLAHBLAH YACKADA YAPPITY FLAPPITY YABBA FLABBA

BIP

NO BUGS IN YOUR FOOD AND NO RATS IN YOUR WALLS AND NO BIG CRIME SURGE AFTER DARK BECAUSE THERE **ISN'T** ANY DARK. JUST SHUT OFF YOUR WINDOWS WHEN YOU DECIDE YOU'VE HAD ENOUGH.

HOURS AND **DAYS** AND **WEEKS**. NICE NEAT AND DEPENDABLE, AND TONS OF THINGS GOING ON TO FILL THOSE HOURS UP, AND A NICE QUIET NEST TO RETREAT BACK TO. NO MORE NEIGHBORHOODS OUT IN THE OPEN WITH BIG WALLS AROUND THEM AND RAZOR WIRE AND BROKEN GLASS ON TOP OF 'EM. NO MORE ARMED GUARDS AND GUNFIRE AT NIGHT. NO MORE LIVING IN A GLORIFIED ROOT CELLAR BECAUSE WE'RE TOO AFRAID TO LIVE IN THE HOUSE ITSELF. EVERYTHING ABOVE GROUND AND I **DON'T** JUST MEAN THE BUILDINGS.

JUST SCHOOL, AND HOME. AND BOOKS AND MOVIES AND A HOT BATH ANYTIME I WANT ONE (!)

PLIK

PLIK

NO MORE WORRYING ABOUT WHETHER IT'S THE WORLD OUT**SIDE** THAT'S INSANE AND DANGEROUS, OR MY FATHER **IN**SIDE THE BASEMENT **WITH** US.

WHAT YOU SEE IS WHAT YOU GET

NO MORE

WEIRD SHIT

UNDER THE SURFACE

PLIK

AND HELP FOR MY LITTLE SISTER MARCIE AND ROOM TO RUN AND SCREAM FOR LYNNE ~

P DEK

AND PEACE AND QUIET AND GOOD MONEY FOR MOM ~

PLIK

ZIP:-

OHGOD OHGOD

SPLAGASSH!

HOOPF! SLOSSH

WHAWAWHAT, KID, **WHAT?**? WHASSA MATTA ?!?

UH-AH-A-WAH-**WHAT'S** GOING ON? ARE YOU **HURT**?

ARE YOU CRAZY?? ALL I KNOW IS I COME IN HERE AND YOU DID IT ON **PUR**POSE TO **SCARE** ME YOU **ASS**~—

CRACK'M WHACK'R SMACK'N

RAE, RAE! CHILL **OUT**!!

RACHEL, IT'S **NOTHING**! IT'S JUST SOMETHING I **LEARNED** A **LONG TIME** AGO, FROM SOME PEOPLE WHO LIVE WAY OUT IN THE **OCEAN**, OKAY? THAT'S HOW THEY **SLEEP** — THEY COME UP FOR AIR EVERY FIFTEEN MINUTES OR SO. IT'S **RELAXING**, OKAY?

ANYBODY CAN LEARN TO DO IT, ALL **RIGHT**?

IT'S **OKAY**, STOP QUIVERIN'. I'M ALL RIGHT. I GUESS I SHOULDA LOCKED THE DOOR, BUT I DIDN'T THINK ANYBODY'D BE AWAKE.

AW~ JEEZ~ YOU'RE GETTING ME ALL W~—

~WHA??

—OH.

WHOOPS.

~HEHH HEH~

STILL A KID AFTER ALL.

THIS IS NOT A DOG.
IT'S A-

DAMN THING

THERE WAS A TIME WHEN I MEANT TO GIVE THE DAMN THING A NAME BUT THERE'S SOMETHING ABOUT THE DAMN THING THAT OFTEN PRECLUDES EVEN THE USE OF PRONOUNS, LET ALONE NAMES.
I DON'T REALLY LIKE HITTING THE DAMN THING. THERE JUST DOESN'T SEEM TO BE ANY OTHER WAY TO GET ITS ATTENTION!

ANYBODY'D SAY, START WITH A CUB, RAISE IT UP RIGHT, AND YOU'LL NEVER HAVE A PROBLEM, BUT **HELL**, THIS **IS** A CUB!

MY RAPPORT WITH THE DAMN THING IS NECESSARY TO MY SURVIVAL.

I DON'T KNOW HOW OR WHY EXACTLY.

I'VE HAD THIS DREAM THOUSANDS OF TIMES. IT COMES UPON ME NOW SOMETIMES EVEN WHEN I'M AWAKE.

= GULP ULP SCARF SMACK =

I'VE TRAINED **DOGS**. **BIG**, AGGRESSIVE DOGS, LITTLE YIP-YIP DOGS, EXOTIC DOGS WITH THREE HEADS AND POISON FANGS. **ALL** OF THEM WERE TRACTABLE AND EASY COMPARED TO THIS **DAMN THING!**

THE DAMN THING'S LIKE A CROSS BETWEEN A JUNKIE AND A TWO-YEAR-OLD, IN A DOG'S SKIN, WITH A CAT'S WAYWARDNESS .... AND A PIG'S PUNGENT REEK!

I SAID, NO BEG.

I SAID **NO,** DAMMIT!

YOU **CAN'T** TIE IT UP OR EVEN SHUT A **DOOR** ON IT. WHAT IT CAN'T UNTIE OR CHEW THROUGH IT'LL BREAK DOWN. IT CHEWED DOWN A FUCKIN' **TREE** TO GET AT FOOD I HUNG FROM A BRANCH!

A CHOKE CHAIN'S NO GOOD. I'M NOT STRONG ENOUGH.

IT'S **BREATH** SMELLS **MOST** DELIGHTFUL FROM ITS FEASTING ON ITS OWN FECES WHICH I'M TOLD IS NECESSARY TO ITS DIGESTION.

I DON'T SEE WHY THIS MAKES YOU SO CRAZY.

I DON'T SEE HOW A MERE ANIMAL CAN BE AS DISRUPTIVE AS YOU SAY.

WHY **CAN'T** YOU CONTROL IT?

WHY CAN'T YOU JUST LET IT HAVE ITS WAY AND RELAX?

WHO'S TRAININ' **WHO** HERE?

YANK YANK YANK

SHLORK SHLORK SHLOP SHLURPP.

HAH HAH HAH HAH HAH

OH, I LET IT HAVE ITS WAY, ALL RIGHT. IT AIN'T AS IF I HAVE MUCH **CHOICE** --BUT AS FOR **RELAXING**-- AS IN, LEARNING TO **LIKE** IT-

--**THEY** DON'T KNOW WHAT I HAVE TO FACE AT NIGHT.

NO **LOCK** WILL CONFOUND IT. NO **DOOR** WILL KEEP IT OUT FOR LONG. NO THREAT AFFECTS IT ONCE MY EYES CLOSE.

IT DOESN'T **JUST** INSIST UPON LAYING NEXT TO ME WHILE I'M ASLEEP.

IT **LICKS** ME, WHEREVER IT CAN GET TO SKIN -AND IT RASPED OFF MY LEATHER OVERCOAT TO GET **AT** ME ONCE -- --IT---

--ITS TONGUE IS HUGE AND FLABBY AND STICKY-WET LIKE A GIANT **SNAIL**. IT DOES THIS ALMOST **EVERY** NIGHT - IT BACKS OFF **ONLY** WHEN I WAKE UP AND **HIT** IT.

I WANNA ASK OTHER PEOPLE **HOW** TO MAKE THE DAMN THING **STOP** BUT I HEARD OF A GUY WHO **NO SHIT** WENT TO **JAIL** FOR "ABUSING" ONE OF THESE THINGS --

AND **THAT** WAS JUST FOR **HITTING IT,** NOT FOR **KILLING IT.**

SO I **CAN'T** TELL ANYBODY ABOUT IT--THEY'D THINK I WAS GETTING **OFF** ON THIS OR SOMETHING...

AFTER ALL, **I'M** THE **MAN; IT'S** JUST AN ANIMAL. - A **DAMN THING**--

I'M SICK ALL THE TIME FROM LIVING WITH THIS DAMN THING. I CAN'T SLEEP, I CAN'T THINK, I CAN'T GET CONTROL OF IT. TOUGH AS IT IS, I'M STILL AFRAID OF INJURING IT.

MY LITTLE HANDBOOK TELLS ME **WHAT** I'M SUPPOSED TO TEACH THE DAMN THING TO DO, BUT IT DOESN'T TELL ME **WHY** DOING THIS IS SO **VITAL** TO MY **SURVIVAL.**

I **CAN'T** RISK SOMEBODY **STEALING** IT. I **NEED** IT. BUT BEFORE **GOD** I WISH I KNEW **WHY.**

I GUESS I **KNEW** THAT EVENTUALLY THE DAMN THING WOULD GET INTO THE STORE HOUSE. **HELL,** WHY **WOULDN'T** IT?

ALL THE FOOD. THE **ONLY** FOOD. ALL I HAD TO GET ME THROUGH THE WINTER. IT ATE **ALL** THE FOOD AND LEFT THIS ONE CONTINUOUS SHIT ON THE STORE HOUSE FLOOR. (**THAT** ONE, IT DECLINED TO EAT.)

SO. NOW I HAD COME TO THE END. I WAS GOING TO STARVE TO DEATH. AND THE DAMN THING WAS GOING TO LIVE.

IT'D HANG AROUND AND BADGER ME; YOWL FOR FOOD, WATCH ME DIE, AND EAT MY BODY WHEN I DID.

I WAS SO RELIEVED I SAT DOWN AND CRIED LIKE A DAMN BABY.

SO I WENT TO MY SHOP IN THE BACK AND BUILT A SMALL DEVICE.

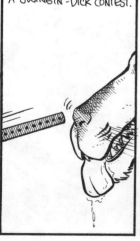

I CAME UPON THE DAMN THING SLEEPING AND JAMMED THE DEVICE INTO ITS LEFT EAR.

IT KICKED AROUND SOME AS THE DEVICE DRILLED THROUGH BONE AND SETTLED PROBES INTO THAT LONG-NEGLECTED AND ATROPHIED PAIN CENTER OF ITS BRAIN. BUT WITH A GOOD SHAKE AND A RESONANT FART IT COMPOSED ITSELF.

THE "STICK" IS A TRANSMITTER; A SIMPLE DESIGN MADE FROM A LENGTH OF CAST-IRON PIPE.

NOW, THEN.

SIT.

SIT.

YEAH, **YOU** KNOW WHAT I'M SAYING.

THAT'S **TWO**.

SIT.

MAGIC NUMBER.

SEE, WHAT WE HAVE HERE IS **NOT** A FAILURE TO COMMUNICATE. IT'S A SWINGIN'-DICK CONTEST.

UP TILL NOW, I HAVEN'T HAD A STAKE IN THE GAME, 'CAUSE I DIDN'T WANT TO GO SO FAR AS TO **INJURE** THE DAMN THING.

NOW IT DOESN'T MATTER IF I **KILL** THE DAMN THING. NOT EVEN TO **ME**. I'M **PAST** THAT.

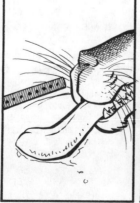

THAT'S ALL THAT MATTERS NOW.

I-- DO NOT-- NEED THIS!

HOUSEFUL OF **YEARS** WORTH OF **JUNK** ALL **GOTTA** GET PACKED UP **TODAY**, AND YOU **KNOW** ALL I GOT FOR **HELP** IS THIS **EQUALLY** USELESS HOUSEFUL OF **ZOMBIES** -

LYNNE GONE **OF COURSE**, MOM "MEDITATING" **OF COURSE**, THE BABY STILL GETTING OVER BEING SICK **OF COURSE**, AND **YOU** DISAPPEAR ON ME, **OF COURSE** !!!

YOU **COME**, YOU **GO**, YOU **DO** ALL THIS **WEIRD SHIT**! YOU LOOK ALL **WOUNDED** WHEN I SAY **MAYBE** I DON'T TRUST **TOTALLY** A GUY WHO THINKS **NOTHIN'** OF BREAKIN' DOWN THE FRICK'N FRONT **DOOR**! AND ALL **I** DO IS **SIT** AROUND AND **WAIT** LIKE A ~~

KNOCK= KNOCK

OH..... **HI**, MRS. RENSIE... NO, NO, WE'RE NOT READY FOR EXIT INSPECTION YET....

YES, UH, IF WE **COULD** RESCHEDULE AGAIN THAT WOULD JUST BE **GREAT**...

UH, **NO**, MOM'S REALLY, REALLY, REALLY, REALLY, UH, BUSY.

SIX O'CLOCK? ~ SHURE. SIX O'CLOCK SHARP. YUP. NO PROBLEM. CLEAN AS A WHISTLE.

YUP. YES MA'AM. THANK YOU MA'AM THANK YOU FOR BEING SOO PATIENT. I KNOW. THANKS. REALLY. UH HUH. NICE DAY.

THERE COMES A TIME WHEN DULL PANIC OVERCOMES **HOT** PANIC. **HOT** PANIC IS USEFUL. YOU CAN LEAP TALL BUILDINGS IN A SINGLE BOUND IN HOT PANIC. **DULL** PANIC MAKES YOU SLOW. THE HOT LEAD IN YOUR VEINS TURNS COLD AND DRAGS YOU DOWN.

WHAT AM I GOING TO DO?

ONLY ONE THING **TO** DO.

ORDER A PIZZA.

HEY!

WHERE YOU HEADED, JAEGER? THERE'S THIS WILD NEW FAD CALLED "SHARING A CAB" ~~

...AAH. TECHNOPHOBE.

...AND HAVING DONE THE PIZZA THING, THE SPELL WAS BROKEN, AND I WENT BACK TO THE BATHROOM AND PACKED UP **EVERYTHING** IN IT, AND SHUT THE DOOR FIRMLY.

ONE ROOM DOWN, AND I WASN'T EVEN THINKING "THIS IS THE LAST TIME I'LL USE THIS ROOM" ANYMORE. A BREAKTHROUGH!

KNOCK KNOCK

"OH, **HI**, JAEGER, YOU'RE **JUST** IN TIME TO DO A **LOT** OF HEAVY LIFTING" ~~

GOOD EVENING, MISS. ARE YOU RACHEL LOCKHART?

UH -- **GROSVENOR.** RACHEL GROSVENOR.

AH YES. THAT'S WHAT I'D LIKE TO SPEAK TO YOU ABOUT.

EXCUSE ME?

IS YOUR MOTHER EMMA LOCKHART ALSO AVAILABLE? I'D LIKE TO SPEAK TO HER AS WELL.

WELL, LADY, I GOTTA ADMIT, I CAN'T FIGURE OUT **WHAT** YOU'RE SELLING.

I BEG YOUR PARDON, MISS. I AM YOUR FATHER'S AUNT.

MISS?

MY FA-- UH

BUT THAT MAKES YOU MY--

I AM YOUR **FATHER'S** AUNT.

WHAT I AM TO YOU IS PRECISELY WHAT I WISH TO DISCUSS. MAY I COME IN?

UH ~~ AH, **NO**, MY MOTHER IS MEDITATING, AND ~~

AH.

WELL, I WOULD NEVER PRESUME UPON A LLAVERAC'S MEDITATIONS. I UNDERSTAND THEY ARE CUSTOMARILY HELD AS INVIOLATE. **BUT** SINCE I HAVE BEEN DENIED HOSPITALITY, I SHALL FOLLOW MEDAWAR CUSTOM AND SPEAK BLUNTLY.

WE -- I AM SPEAKING FOR THE GROSVENOR FAMILY SPECIFICALLY-- WE WISH **YOU** AND YOUR MOTHER AND YOUR SIBLINGS TO REASSUME YOUR MOTHER'S FAMILY NAME OF LOCKHART.

WHAT?

WHY?

WE PRESUME THAT YOU FOUR HAVE NO INTENTION OF ACCEPTING BRIGHAM GROSVENOR AS HEAD OF THE HOUSEHOLD, HUSBAND AND FATHER, **SHOULD** HE WISH TO REASSUME THIS ROLE UPON HIS RELEASE FROM PRISON?

WELL-1-1-- HADN'T-- THOUGHT ABOUT--

IF THAT IS THE **CASE**, THERE IS **NO** ADVANTAGE TO YOU IN RETAINING OUR NAME. **NOR** TO HIM.

NOR TO **US**.

IN **FACT**, IF I MAY BE **BOLD** AS WELL AS BLUNT, **YOU** IN PARTICULAR ARE **FAR** BETTER OFF UNDER YOUR MOTHER'S NAME. YOU RESEMBLE YOUR MOTHER'S CLAN VERY STRONGLY INDEED.

YOU SHOULD HAVE QUITE A GOOD CHANCE OF BEING ACCEPTED BY THEM. YOU'D HAVE A BRIGHT FUTURE AHEAD OF YOU. WE'D **ALL** HAVE A BETTER CHANCE OF PUTTING ASIDE ...YOUR PARENTS' FOLLY.

MY PARENTS **WEREN'T**--

STOP.

THINK OF THE PAIN IT HAS CAUSED TO THEM. TO **YOU**.

YOUR LIFE **CAN'T** HAVE BEEN EASY. IT IS TIME NOW TO SMOOTH IT OVER. IF YOU WILL.

GOOD NIGHT.

UH!

NEVER EVEN TOLD ME HER **NAME** ...

CLOSED **MY** FRONT DOOR **HERSELF** ...

126

DOWNING
STREET
NEXT

SKO

HERE YA GO, BUD; TWELVE-FIFTY AND YOU'RE A FREE MAN.

Smudko's
DOESN'T REALLY TASTE
LESS YOU'RE AFRAID
IT'LL KILL YOU"

SURE YOU DON'T WANT ME TO STICK AROUND? THIS BEIN' A CLAN NEIGHBORHOOD, AND NOT **YOUR** CLAN, I MEAN ─

I DON'T RECALL ASKIN' **YOU** A **GOD DAMN THING!**

OKAY, OKAY-- COP-FACE **JERK!**

"IT DO...
GOOD UN...
IT MIGHT...ILL YOU"

SKOPTS

CLAN OR **NO** CLAN.

NONE OF 'EM CAN COMPARE TO MY EMMA.

I SHOULD **WOR**-RY
I SHOULD **CARE**
I SHOULD MAR-RY
A MILL-ION-AIRE

HE SHOULD DIE I SHOULD CRY I SHOULD MAR-RY ANOTHER GUY

SIGH

I LOOK LIKE A LLAVERAC UNTIL I SMILE.

MY FATHER WAS ~ IS ~ A MEDAWAR. MILITARY MAN, LIKE MOST OF 'EM.

I GREW UP IN A MEDAWAR TOWN. THEY NEVER LIKED **ME** AND I CAN'T SAY I EVER LIKED **THEM.**

MY **MOTHER** IS, OR **WAS,** A LLAVERAC.

I ALWAYS PICTURED THEM AS THESE GAUZY ROMANTIC PRINCESSES AND THAT MY MOM AND I WOULD GO LIVE WITH **THEM** SOMEDAY AND LIFE WOULD BE GREAT.

NOW IN **SPITE** OF THE FACT THAT **THAT** BUBBLE WAS **WELL** AND TRULY POPPED, OUR WHOLE FUTURE DEPENDS ON MY GETTING INTO THE LLAVERACS WHEN I'M TWENTY-ONE. SHE'D BE ABSOLVED, MY KID SISTERS COULD GO TO COLLEGE.

I'D BE ON **EASY** STREET.

SKRIKK

WE CAME **HERE,** WHERE THE **ENTIRE** CITY GUARD ARE MEDAWARS ~ BECAUSE IT'S **ALSO** THE LLAVERAC CLAN HOME.

BUT EVERY ONCE IN A WHILE I SEE ONE OF **THEM** WHO SOMEHOW LOOKS MORE LIKE **HIM** THAN ALL THE OTHERS.

IT'S **NOT** LIKE I DON'T **KNOW** THAT'S A LOONEY IDEA. I **KNOW** WHAT WOULD HAPPEN IF I **DID.**

HE'D LOOK ME UP AND DOWN WITH THAT AWFUL STONE FACE THEY GET AND THINK I WAS JUST SOME HISTRIONIC LLAVERAC HAVING A FIT~.

AND I WANT TO GO UP TO HIM AND SAY, MISTER, MY DADDY WAS A MEDAWAR, AND HE'S IN PRISON NOW, AND I KIND OF HOPE HE **STAYS** THERE, BUT IF HE WAS HERE RIGHT NOW I'D PROBABLY FORGIVE HIM FOR ALL THE THINGS HE DID TO US, AND COULD I JUST HOLD YOUR HAND AND CRY JUST A LITTLE BIT?

~OR TRYING TO **ROB** HIM OR **HIT** ON HIM OR **WHO KNOWS** WHAT--

--HE'D JUST GET THAT **SMIRK** AND TURN AWAY WITH A SCORNFUL SNORT--

--AND I'D JUST WANT TO SMASH HIS **TEETH** IN--

--BUT **JUST** AS I GET **REALLY** STEAMED (WHICH **DOESN'T** FEEL **THAT** MUCH BETTER THAN **PINING** BUT I'LL **TAKE** IT)--

--THIS LITTLE TRICKLE OF FEAR STOPS ME COLD AND I THINK---

--MAYBE THIS **IS** DAD.

MAYBE IT'S **REALLY HIM** AND HE'S ONLY **PRETENDING** NOT TO KNOW ME.

MAYBE HE'S BEEN **FOLLOWING** ME, TRYING TO FIND OUT WHERE WE **LIVE.**

HE'S **SUPPOSED** TO BE IN **PRISON** FOR **YEARS** YET, A LOOONG, **LONG** WAY AWAY FROM HERE.

BUT IF HE GOT OUT **EARLY,** WOULD HIS FAMILY TELL **US?**

....MAYBE **NOT.**

MAYBE, I THINK, MAYBE **HE** DOESN'T KNOW **ME.** I LOOK LIKE A LLAVERAC. MY BEST HOPE IS TO STICK WITH MY MOTHER'S PEOPLE (EVEN THOUGH I **LOATHE** THEM.) USE MY NATURAL CAMOUFLAGE.

AND WIPE THAT SMILE OFF MY FACE.

KNOCK KNOCK

DRRRRGH!

AAH, TURN **BLUE**. I GOT **WORK** TO DO.

WHIMPER

SSHH, MARCIE. HE'LL **HEAR** YOU.

KNOCK-KNOCK

HE'LL HEAR YOU
HE'LL HEAR
HE'LL HE
HE'LL

KNOCK = KNOCK

BOUND

MOM!
MOM!

STUDIO KEEP OUT

TAP TAP

♪ LET'S RUB NOSES LIKE THE ES-KI-MO-SES ♪

DON'T CHA KNOW THAT'S ES-KI-MO FOR "I LOVE YOU"

TYPE TYPE

KEEP OUT

KNOCK-KNOCK

SSHACCC

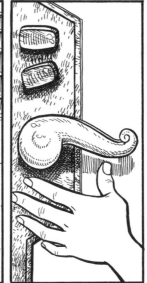

GADAAH!

THUMP!

HEY! **NICE** ELEVATION!

WHERE THE HECK DID **YOU** COME FROM??

I **KNOCKED**, DIDN'T I?

KNOCK-KNOCK

WELL **WHO'S** KNOCKIN' **NOW**??

HEH!

JUST SOME GUYS I KNOW. I FIGURED YOU'ER IN THE **TUB** OR SOMETHIN', SO—

CUTE KID!

SO, YOU'D JUST SCARE THE BILLY BEJESUS OUT OF ME, HUH?

AWWW, HONEY...

AWWWW, HONEY!

AND WHERE'VE YOU **BEEN?** YOU **KNEW** WE HAD—

TAKIN' THE FIRST LOAD, WHAT ELSE?

NOT TO MENTION THE DUMPSTER LOAD ALL THAT JUNK YOUR MAMA **FINALLY** AGREED TO LET **GO** OF?

AHH...

GHOD, THAT FEELS **SO** GOOD... WHAT A **HOME**COMING....

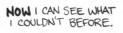

NOW I CAN SEE WHAT I COULDN'T BEFORE.

I WAS SO PARANOID, ALL I COULD THINK WAS HOW ALL THIS COULD'VE BEEN FAKED-UP SOMEHOW.

BUT **NOW** I CAN SEE THAT THERE **ARE** THINGS HERE THAT **COULDN'T** BE ANYBODY ELSE'S.

THANK GOD FOR THE KIDS. THEIR FACES SHOW SIGNS OF **MINE**, THAT CAN'T **EVER** BE ERASED OR DENIED.

PROVE WHAT?

BRIGHAM, I **LOVE** YOU — DON'T **TRY** SO HARD!

WELL, I **GOT** TO TRY HARD **NOW**. DAMN HARD.

HELL, WHAT WOMAN'D WASTE HER TIME **BELIEVIN'** THAT OLD "OH, IT'S ALL **DIFFERENT** NOW, I'M A **CHANGED** MAN, TAKE ME **BACK**" CRAP?

WHAT **MAN'D RESPECT** HER IF SHE **DID**?

HELL'S BELLS, I GOTTA **CLEAN** THIS PLACE **UP**!

SHIT, I **HOPE** I DIDN'T BREAK ANYTHING SHE REALLY **LIKED**...

I'M **SORRY,** I'M **SORRY** EMMA, IT WAS ONLY 'CAUSE I WAS REALLY **TENSE**...

TALK'S NOT GONNA CONVINCE HER. I GOT TO **SHOW** HER I'M IN A GOOD GROOVE NOW, THAT I **CAN** GET BETTER, THAT EVERYTHING **CAN** BE FIXED....

HOW HOW **HOW**..

EMMA, I NEVER THOUGHT THIS WOULD BE **EASY.** I NEVER **WANTED** IT TO BE EASY.

I **BELIEVE** IN REDEMPTION. I **KNOW** DESPITE EVERYTHING THAT IT'S POSSIBLE.

RISING RD E

010110

SO RAKE ME OVER THE COALS, BABY. I **WANT** IT.

MONEY. YEAH.

IT'S **ALL** GOING TO **HER** FROM NOW **ON.**

I WON'T EVEN LOOK TO SEE HOW **MUCH** IT IS. A TRIBUTE.

FOR MY FORGIVENESS.

FOR MY JOY.

GOT TO GET 'EM A NEW **HOUSE.**

YEAH. THIS PLACE IS TOO MUCH LIKE THAT

(cell)

CELLAR WE LIVED IN WAY BACK WHEN. NO ROOM FOR THREE GROWING KIDS, **FORGET** ROOM TO PATCH UP A ROMANCE.

IT'S NOT ENOUGH.

WHAT'S NEEDED HERE IS A **SACRIFICE.**

I'LL LEAVE HER MY FREE-MAN LICENSE.

I'M SUPPOSED TO KEEP IT ON ME **ALWAYS.** IF I GOT CAUGHT **WITHOUT** IT, VWOOOP, BACK TO PRISON.

AND **SHE'D** HAVE TO **BRING** IT TO ME, MAKE **EXCUSES** FOR ME, GET ME SPRUNG. **SAVE** ME, AS I'D SAVE **HER.**

PERFECT. **THAT'LL** SHOW HER I **TRUST** HER.

MOM— I THINK I FOUND THE LAST OF DAD'S OLD CRUD!

OH?

—SORRY, AVERY—

RACHEL, JUST— Y'KNOW— DEFENESTRATE.

I'M HERE, AVE —YOU SURE YOU GUYS NEED SO BIG A TRUCK? I REALLY WANT TO GET RID OF A LOT MORE...

AI~YA~YAAHH... JUST LIKE THAT?

'I I' LIKE IT!'

ALL THIS CRAP WE'VE BEEN CARTIN' AROUND LIKE A DEATH SENTENCE ALL THESE YEARS....

..GONE, GONE, GONE!

OW.

JAEGER?

WHAT THE HECK ARE YOU DOING IN THERE, MONSTER MAN??

JUS' TAKIN' A BREAK IS ALL.

IN THE DUMPSTER?

PERF'CLY COMFORTABLE.

YEAH, AS LONG AS I'M NOT THROWIN' AWAY ANYTHING NASTY!

YEAH, IT'S OKAY TO THROW OUT PERFECTLY GOOD SOCKET-WRENCH SETS?

IT'S HIS, ISN'T IT?

OKAY, KID.

'SCUSE ME, GENTS.

TAP TAP

YEAH?

SORRY TO BOTHER YOU. I'M INQUIRING ON BEHALF OF THE FIRST CHURCH OF HUITZILIPOCHTLI RELEASING COMPANY REGARDING SOME FOOTAGE SHOT IN THIS AREA LAST MONTH.

WHOA, WHOA — **WE'RE** JUST THE **MOVERS.** THE FOLKS WHO **LIVE** HERE **AIN'T** HERE.

YOU'RE LOCALS, THOUGH, AREN'T YOU?

—YEAH— SURE.

WELL, YOU MAY HAVE SEEN THIS FILM ON THE BIGGER PIRATE TV STATIONS OVER THE LAST THREE WEEKS.

OH YEAH THAT'S THE LITTLE GODSFEAST TAVERN.

mm.fall.doc

SHEE—**YIT,** THEY **STILL** AIN'T GOT THAT BIG WINDOW FIXED.

YOU'RE FAMILIAR WITH THE PLACE?

'COURSE. BUT I WADN'T **IN** THERE WHEN IT HAPPENED. WHAT **DID—**

YOW!

mm.fall.doc

YEP. NOW, **ALL** FILM BELONGS IN THE PUBLIC DOMAIN FOR ITS FIRST MONTH OF EXISTENCE. THAT TIME'S ALMOST UP NOW, AND OWNERSHIP WILL REVERT TO THE PEOPLE DEPICTED AND TO WHOEVER SHOT THE FILM. FIRST CHURCH WANTS TO BUY IT FROM THEM FOR THEIR STOCK FOOTAGE LIBRARY.

BUT YOU SEE, THEY CAN'T FIND **THIS** MAN, TO OBTAIN HIS PERMISSION TO USE HIS LIKENESS.

mm.fall.doc

unknown

SHEE — IT'S SIX STOREYS DOWN ON **THAT** SIDE. YOU **AIN'T** GONNA FIND 'IM.

HUH! NOT OUTSIDE 'A A **DUMPSTER,** ANYWAY.

AAOW! MAN!
AW, HE'S **TOAST.**

mm.doc.fall

unknown

WELL, THE **OTHER** MEN INVOLVED IN THE ACCIDENT **DID** DIE ON IMPACT. BUT **THEY'VE** ALL BEEN IDENTIFIED AND THEIR FAMILIES' CONSENT OBTAINED.

SORRY WE DON'T HAVE A BETTER HEAD SHOT THAN **THIS.**

mm.doc.fall

enhance 600+

THIS MAN VANISHED FROM THE SCENE WITHIN MINUTES OF HITTING LOCH RAVEN FREEWAY. NO IDEA **HOW,** WHERE **TO,** OR WITH WHOSE **HELP.**

ANY INFORMATION THAT LEADS TO OUR FINDING THIS GUY OR WHOEVER SHOT THIS FILM WILL BE **WELL** PAID FOR BY THE FIRST CHURCH OF HUITZILI-POCHTLI RELEASING COMPANY.

SORRY MAN, CAN'T HELP YA.

I BET 'E'S **GONE.** YA'LL MIGHT AS WELL GO ON 'N MAKE YOUR MOVIE.

HEH! WISH WE COULD, BUT IT'S NOT ORTHODOX.

H'MM- WELL, IF HE'S **NOT** DEAD, I DOUBT **SERIOUSLY** HE STILL LOOKS LIKE **THAT!** SO YOU CAN SELL HIS **OLD** LIKENESS. NO PROBLEM!

WELL, THANKS ANY WAY. OH— THE FAMILY THAT LIVES HERE, HAVE YOU GOT A FORWARDING ADDRESS ?

HUH?

OH. SURE.

THERE YA GO.

SECRET GARDENS
LANDSCAPING & GARDEN DESIGN
MA GROSVENOR
OIOIIO RISING RD E
8220-2706-8787-02 AI

HEY!

WHAT?

TRA... ONLY"
NO B... REFUSE"
NO FUR...TURE.

WELL, MONSTER MAN, LOOKS LIKE YOU **OWE** US ONE !

OH, YEAH? OWE YOU ONE **WHAT?**

OH—**JUST A BEER.**

OH. JUST A **BEER.** NO PROBLEM.

138

SO, JAEGER MONSTER.

I B'LIEVE I NEED SOME PERSPECTIVE.

WHAT'S THE STORY HERE?

GREENTREE APTS.

fountainbleu apts.

ASILOMAR ACRES

VISTA VILLES

Dunroami

NO STORY TO IT. JUST HELPIN' OUT A LADY.

≡ SNIFFK ≡

YOU SURE ABOUT THE LADY PART? SHE IS LLAVERAC CLAN, ISN'T SHE?

HA! SURE. WELL, SHE'S A LADY WHERE IT COUNTS, THAT'S ALL.

HEH!

SO. SHE'S YOUR LADY THEN.

OH, I DUNNO. KIND OF UP TO HER, AIN'T IT?

UH HUH. AND HOW 'BOUT THE LITTLE ONE?

RACHEL? SHE'S A KID.

HAW HAW HAW! NOT IN MY NEIGHBORHOOD!

NOT IN **YOUR** NEIGHBORHOOD, EITHER, FROM WHAT **I** UNDERSTAND. AIN'T IT "OLD ENOUGH TO BLEED IS OLD ENOUGH TO BREED"?

YOU'RE A **PIG**, CYN.

WE-E-E-LL, TRUTH BE TOLD, ONCE A KID **THAT** AGE MAKES UP HER MIND, YOU **KNOW** YOU CAN'T TELL HER A DAMN **THING**.

HA HAHA HA~ OHH YEAH!

BUT CITY KIDS ARE KINDA **STUPID** THAT WAY. **OH NO.** I BEEN DOWN **THAT** ROAD. I DON'T WANT ANY **MORE** OF **THAT** CRAZY SHIT.

≡SNFF≡

SLAM!

HI, GUYS! WE'RE BACK!

OH, THE NEW PLACE IS **SO** GORGEOUS!

SCRRIIIIIITJ...

HEY, LOOK HOW MUCH **ROOM** THERE IS IN HERE WITH ALL OUR **JUNK** OUT OF IT! WOW!

RAE! C'MERE AND HELP ME A MINUTE!

COMING, MOM!

≡SNICCKK≡

≡SNRK≡

WAHAHAHAHA HAWHA...

STILL DON'T WANNA GET ANY MORE O' THAT ??

HAAHA

DOES THAT MEAN YOU DON'T LIKE **ME?**

WHAT? OF **COURSE** NOT, MARCIE. I **LOVE** YOU.

BUT **YOU** SAID YOU LIKE GUYS MORE THAN GIRLS, AND **I'M** A GIRL.

IT'S NOT QUITE LIKE **THAT,** SIS. IT'S A WEIRD GROWN-UP THING. WHAT I **MEAN** IS, I FEEL MORE AT **HOME** WITH MEN THAN WITH WOMEN.

GUYS ARE.... MORE **HONEST,** SOMEHOW.

ALTHOUGH **YEAH,** A LOT OF THEM **DO** LIE TO GET WHAT THEY WANT...

I DUNNO, IT'S HARD TO EXPLAIN.

NO MATTER **HOW** MUCH THEY CUSS AND DRINK AND SPIT AND SCRATCH THEMSELVES, I **STILL** LIKE 'EM BETTER THAN ♪LLLLADIES♪ WHO ARE **JUST** AS **MEAN** AND UNLOVELY, BUT **THEY** GET ALL **PIOUS** IF YOU **CALL** THEM ON IT.

WHAT? YOU **USED** TO BE A LOT MORE LIKE A BOY **YOURSELF.** YOU AND LYNNE USED TO BE **FRIENDS.**

NOW YOU WEAR A DRESS AND MAKE-UP PRACTICALLY **EVERY** DAY. HOW COME, IF YOU DON'T LIKE LADIES?

≡SIGH≡

PROBABLY BECAUSE I CAN'T **BE** A GUY MYSELF, AND THE OLDER YOU GET, THE LESS GUYS KNOW WHAT TO **SAY** TO YOU IF YOU DON'T—...

OHH, I DON'T KNOW, BABY. I WISH I DID.

HEY, **WHO** SPRUNG FOR THE HOT DEAD BIRD?

YEARS OF ENJOYMENT

GROTESQUE IMAGE

OH FOR CRYING OUT LOUD

WHH!! YOU'LL GIVE THE KIDS **COMPLEXES**.

OH IT'S A HARMLESS TREAT REALLY

HUH! IF ONLY IT **WAS** REAL MEAT.

I THINK YOU STREET-CRAWLERS WOULD BE **WAY** BETTER OFF IF YOU ATE **SOME**THING BESIDES THIS **FAKE**

SHEEP DOG? "OH, KETTLE, THOU ART SO **BLACK!**" THE POT EXCLAIMS!

WE-**HELL**, LOOK WHO IT IS?!

GOOD **TIMING**, LYNNE, WE'RE OUTTA HERE **AND** YOU DIDN'T HAVE TO **LIFT** ANYTHIN'

AAH....

ROOM ENOUGH TO SWING A RUG-MONKEY...

DON'T YOU THINK THOSE **GANGSTERS** SCARE **ME**, EMMA GROSVENOR, YOU ARROGANT FULLBLOOD YOU'RE **STILL** NOT GETTING YOUR SECURITY DEPOSIT BACK OR

OH, KEEP IT, LUDIE, **DO**. BUY YOURSELF A **LIFE**.

FLIK!

OKAY, SAY "BYE, MOUSE-HOLE"!

ASILOMAR ACRES
Dunroamin
apts

WHAT A **PERFECT** DAY!

S̶M̶I̶T̶H̶

AAAAAAA!!

143

NE KULTURNY. IT'S "I WENT TO THE WOODS BECAUSE I WANTED TO LIVE DELIBERATELY.

"I WANTED TO LIVE DEEP AND SUCK OUT ALL THE MARROW OF LIFE.

"TO PUT TO ROUT ALL THAT WAS NOT LIFE

"AND NOT, WHEN I CAME TO DIE, DISCOVER THAT I HAD NOT LIVED."

HOT HOT

TOO HOT. ROUGH CLOTH. SQUEAK-SQUEAK-SQUEAK-SQUEAK-SQUEAK

SMELL OF SWEAT AND SPOILED FOOD. SILVER BARS PAINFULLY BRIGHT

WHINING, COMPLAINING VOICES

MOTHER'S VOICE STRANGE, HIGH AND FLUTING. NOT COMPLETELY SOOTHING.

DUST AND SAND.

THEN COLD

WARM WIND

SILVER BARS NOW TOO COLD TO TOUCH.

STARS TOO NEAR MOON TOO BRIGHT.

HISSING SOUND RISES TO A ROAR

SMELL OF BURNING GRASS TASTE OF STALE WATER HIGH WHINE OF INSECTS, RISING AND FALLING

GOING ON, AND ON, AND ON, AND ON, AND ON.

PSSST!

MARS.

IT'S OKAY THIS TIME. THIS TIME WE'VE GOT SOME WHERE TO GO.

mmf. JUST LET ME OUT HERE.

OKAY.

"OUT"?

ON THE STREET?

IN THIS?

SURE. I GOT THINGS TO DO.

BUT THERE'S A NICE SEALED GARAGE AT THE NEW PLACE. WHY DO YOU HAVE TO GET OUT HERE?

MARCIE, STAY DOWN, HONEY. I'M JUST MOVING OVER.

AAH, IT AIN'T GONNA KILL YA.

≡OUUGHH!≡ CLOSE THAT REEKHOLE!

≡AWGH≡!

ACTUALLY, THESE FOGS DO KILL PEOPLE—

—BUT—.

OH, LET HIM, LET HIM. GO ON, AVERY, DRIVE.

O·bee·KAY·bee...

FROM THE GUT.

sniffFFFFFFFF

VRRRMm...

U-ROB

≡HAAAAHHH≡

THUMPA THUMPA THUMPA

SNERFF OH YEAH.

CINNAMON and CANNABIS DRIFTING IN THE HAZE

CONSIDER THE SENSE OF SMELL.

A LITTLE BROWNSKIN GIRL HE'D HAD, A LONG TIME AGO, BUT NOT LONG ENOUGH AGO...

SWEET TINKLY LAUGH

GREEDY LITTLE thing....

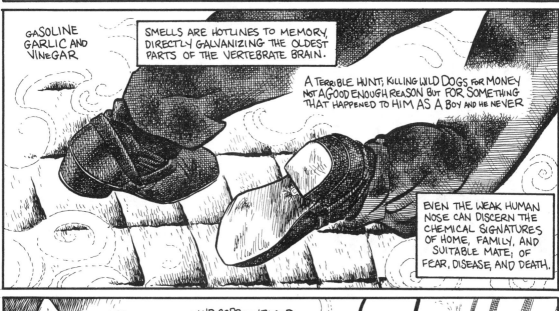

GASOLINE GARLIC AND VINEGAR

SMELLS ARE HOTLINES TO MEMORY, DIRECTLY GALVANIZING THE OLDEST PARTS OF THE VERTEBRATE BRAIN.

A TERRIBLE HUNT, KILLING WILD DOGS FOR MONEY NOT A GOOD ENOUGH REASON BUT FOR SOMETHING THAT HAPPENED TO HIM AS A BOY AND HE NEVER

EVEN THE WEAK HUMAN NOSE CAN DISCERN THE CHEMICAL SIGNATURES OF HOME, FAMILY, AND SUITABLE MATE; OF FEAR, DISEASE, AND DEATH.

HOT WATER WARM MILK AND COPPERY BLOOD

TO CREATURES MORE DEFINITIVELY RULED BY THE SENSE OF SMELL, AN OVER-WHELMING STEW OF ODORS IS A POWER-FUL INTOXICANT

PROMPTING ACTION WITHOUT THOUGHT, BODIES JOLTING AND HYPERREACTIVE.

HOME WITH FATHER ALIVE AND MARTHA HAPPY

SULFUR, DARK COFFEE AND RANK HORSE SWEAT

THE AIR OF THE DOME-CITY OF ANVARD (WHICH IS NOT SO MUCH ENCLOSED BY ITS DOME AS RESTRAINED AND SHAPED BY IT) IS POISONOUSLY RICH.

OUT ON THE STEPPES, BITTERLY COLD. MOST OF THE SOLDIERS FROZE TO DEATH AND HE COULDN'T UNDERSTAND WHY

THE EXHALATIONS OF BUSINESS AND MANUFACTORY AND HUNDREDS OF THOUSANDS OF PEOPLE SIMMER INTO A RICH POLYATMOS.

RANCID GREASE, AMMONIA, A GOATY SMELL THAT ISN'T GOAT

MACHINES SCRUB THIS CHEMICAL STAIN INTO A FAINT RESIDUE, MEANT FOR LESS ROBUST PALATES.

PRISON
CHIPPED PAINT
OLD STEEL
STALE WATER

THE RESULTING DISTILLATE IS OF COURSE DUMPED INTO THE RIVER, WHICH FLUSHES THE OCEAN VIVIDLY RED FOR MILES BEYOND THE RIVER'S MOUTH. IT IS NOT EXACTLY POISONOUS BY THEN.

JAEGER TRAVELS, CURIOUSLY SPLIT BETWEEN DELIRIUM AND CLARITY.

HE KNOWS EXACTLY WHAT HE IS GOING.

(DREAMILY)
AS HE FALLS

(SEVERAL HUNDRED YARDS)

HE IS SUDDENLY STRUCK BY A THOUGHT

(THIS RIVER BETTER BE AS DEEP AS I REMEMBER IT)

CITY PEOPLE SAY PINK OR BLUE TO DESIGNATE INFANTS AS FEMALE OR MALE.

PEOPLE OF THE BARRENS USE RED OR WHITE

BUT ONLY IN ADULTHOOD; THE GENDERS OF CHILDREN MATTER LITTLE TO THEM.

HE FALLS

FROM WHITE

INTO

RED.

OH, I'M **WRETCHED**, **PER**FECTLY **WRETCHED**. SAY SOMETHING SWEET TO ME, DEAR.

DADDY, DARLING.

Misc

MISC. Mi: Misc Misc Misc Misc Misc Misc Misc Misc Misc Misc Misc Misc Misc Misc Misc Misc Misc Misc Misc

AH, EMMA. **PEARL** OF MY MISSPENT YOUTH.

RESIDENTS NEAR THE RIVER ARE ACCUSTOMED NOT TO OPEN THEIR WINDOWS, IF THEY HAVE THEM.

IN MOST TOWNS, FEW PEOPLE LOOK **UP**. NEAR THIS RIVER, FEW PEOPLE LOOK **OUT**.

THE COURSE IS STRANGE, AS ALWAYS. DANGER LIES IN BOREDOM AND CERTAINTY.

WHAT'S THIS? PINING AWAY AFTER MOTHER'S PRETTY YOUNG THING?

SWEET RACHEL. HOW ALIKE WE ARE, WE THREE.

Misc Misc Misc Misc Misc Misc Misc Misc Misc Misc Misc Misc Misc Misc Misc Misc Misc Misc Misc Misc Misc Misc Misc Misc Misc

PASSING THE MAIN WINDOWS OF THE "GOLDEN FRITILLARY", HE FINDS HIMSELF WONDERING WHY IT SEEMS SO EASY TO MOVE WITHOUT BEING SEEN.

AS ALWAYS, THE THOUGHT DISCONCERTS HIM, AND HE SHIFTS HIS COURSE TO A MORE DIFFICULT ONE.

OH, **RACHEL**. THERE'S **NO** POINT IN YOUR TYING YOURSELF UP IN KNOTS OVER JAEGER. YOU **KNOW** HE ONLY STAYS AWAY LONG ENOUGH TO MAKE YOU **MAD**.

SO YOU'RE SAYING, IF I DON'T GET MAD, HE'LL STOP GOING **AWAY?** COME **ON**--

"**NO**, IF YOU DON'T GET MAD, SOONER OR LATER HE'LL STOP COMING **BACK**.

"BUT THE WHOLE THING'LL HURT CONSIDERABLY LESS."

"AFTER **ALL**, HE'S A FREE MAN, ISN'T HE? DON'T YOU FIND YOU PREFER HIM THAT WAY?"

NOTES
ON THE PRECEDING

INSIDE ENDPAPER
Inspired by the engravings and watercolors of David Roberts. This was drawn from Abu Simbel, when it was still full of sand. Animal on the left is a male Nyima named Kohut.

PAGE 1
Ganesha, Hindu deity. Hailed as the Remover of Obstacles, he is to be addressed at the beginning of any new venture.

PAGE 2
Jaeger (pronounced Yae'-gurr). He is the first of several Finders. He's much like an Indian scout or detective.

PAGE 3
First blood sacrifice. Ganesha is usuallu honored with fruit or candy, but this is all he's got.

PAGE 5
Trading post—these mark the outermost boundaries of the territory of the city of Anvard.

PAGES 6-7
City of Anvard, seen from the eastern road. The city fills up its dome rather than spread out on the tide plains. An almost unbreakable latticework inside and fixed to the dome serves as building foundation.

In the foreground is Mount Cino, (Chee'noe), topped by a fortified lookout which is an example of the oldest existing structures in Anvard. Cino is riddled with tunnels.

The name 'Anvard' came from a kingdom in the books of C. S. Lewis.

PAGE 8
'Her Majesty's a Pretty Nice Girl'—the Beatles, Abbey Road. The LP was more fun.

Those mecha-suits aren't suits; they're remotely-operated robots. First reference to Hayao Miyazaki's TOTORO. The suits appear only at the perimeter gates of the city or at severe trouble-spots.

The free market—many of the city's population are resident and transient non-citizens. The free markets, mostly found on the lowest levels, are the only places they can buy, sell, and barter legally with full citizens. The full citizens have their own troubles with permits, ID, and accounting; most go to the Markets if they can to get away from paperwork.

Lettering on the banner, left to right, is Arabic, English, Miremai (a trader's language, like Swahili) and Laeske (the big feathery lizards).

Panel 5. Gilroy Garlic doll. Gilroy, California—garlic Capitol of the USA. Won't do you no good to roll your windows up when driving through.

Jaeger's hand-made leathers are ludicrously valuable in urban areas; very expensive and only barely legal.

PAGE 9
Panel 2. Ron Chitin's rookie card? Ron Chitin is a four-armed ex-hockey goalie from Evan Dorkin's PIRATE CORP$! (renamed HECTIC PLANET).

Panel 3. Fat man with parrot is Sidney Greenstreet, as Senor Ferrari, in CASABLANCA.

There are hundreds of TV channels in Anvard. It takes armies of busybodies with cameras and computers to fill 'em up. Careful what you sing in the shower; somebody will consider it an audition.

Free Traders are members of large, ill-defined tribes of nomadic and semi-nomadic people, recognized by law as being able to buy and sell within the cities. They are exempted from carrying ID or permits, but they may not own any real estate, storefront, or permanent dwelling, nor may they receive what is considered a living wage for work. Some breeze in with goods to sell and then back out; others move tent-towns in and out of alleyways, dumpster-diving as they go. They're the first to be hassled whenever trouble starts.

PAGES 10, 11
Whiskey Jack is a victim of a peculiar sexually transmitted disease commonly called the Fey Plague. It randomly inserts animal genes into human bodies, and sometimes vice-versa. It kills most, but is also believed to impart oracular abilities. The little girl with him is his 'rememberer', an attendant with a perfect memory trained to recall every addled word the poor man says.

PAGE 12
Tour guide. Members of her clan are very long-lived, and are as such de facto historians. Her personal name is Medina.

PAGE 15
Panel 2. Inspired by the remarkable photography of Rene-Jacques, in this case ESCALIER A' MONTMARTRE.

PAGE 16
The bookstore is named for the infamous Madame Marie Laveau, Voodoo Mombo.

PAGE 17
Hulger, male Nyima. Many folk in Anvard have animal characteristics in some way or another. Most common are 'constructs' or living artifacts, genetically constructed servants or sex toys mostly. Least common are survivors of the Fey Plague like Whiskey Jack. Somewhere in the middle are such as the Nyima, the centaurs or halfhorses, the Huldres, and so on. They are often treated with the same casual contempt as the constructs, and are very touchy about it.

'Nyima' is a phonetic play on 'Nemea', as in 'Nemean Lion'.

PAGE 18
Bookshop counter-slugs: Virgill, Gyles clan. Ann Handler, manager; Shingtown clan. Miss Lennie, owner; Llaverac clan. Almost all full citizens of Anvard are members of or employed by the clans. Here on the lower levels, the clans mix more comfortably, and non-clan people are better tolerated.

PAGE 19
Panel 4. Why do we see Miss Lennie in her youth? Oh, lots of reasons; but that would be telling.

PAGE 20
Panel 3. The thing in the jar? He wasn't nice.

PAGE 22, PANEL 2
No matter who looks into it, that mirror always reflects the face of the lady who first owned it.

PAGE 23
The Sad Fate of Bob Plant, who was my studio mate for years. Big Areca Palm. Lots of Vitamin C, I guess.

PAGE 25
The river, once it gets within the confines of the city, becomes blood-red.

Panel 3. Spalding Gray, from SWIMMING TO CAMBODIA.

Panel 9. Camera brats from the market. The girl's name is Ruth; she's half Medawar clan and half Heinz-57. The halfhorse boy's name is Kalif (ka LEEF'); he mans the camera.

PAGE 27, 28
Emma and her youngest daughter Marcie. Emma is of Llaverac clan, but her kids are half Medawar clan. Most of the clans are not very tolerant of cross-clan marriage, these two in particular.

PAGE 29
Mount Cino, and Anvard, many thousands of years ago when it was a fortified town.

The absurdly large banner pinned to the side of the mountain depicts a Roman soldier's helmet. Jaeger always dreams of mazes and puzzles.

PAGE 31
Arrow with chevrons is an aviator's symbol indicating severe turbulence

ahead. The banner, which changed from a soldier's helmet to the number 36,now shows a total eclipse. The marks above the doors are hobo code. The sands underfoot are composed of tiny, tiny bones.

PAGE 32
Meet Emma Grosvenor's kids. Rachel, fourteen; Lynne, ten; Marcie, six. Rachel's tall for her age, Marcie's small for hers, and Lynne far too devious for anybody's good. Marcie is the only person in the world Lynne will admit to giving a shit about.

PAGE 37
'Sawing For Teens'— watch more Canadian cartoons. I recommend Richard Condie's stuff in particular.

PAGE 38
Tessa Jhara, Nyiman noblewoman. She's in town working on a medical degree. She would never be granted a license to practice within the city, but she won't need it back home. Ann Handler has it pretty bad for Tessa, who's the jock of her dreams.

Long-haired clerk: Lydia, who was out when Jaeger stopped by the previous day.

PAGE 40
Lynne knows Jaeger has a terrible blind spot for electronics. He doesn't understand them or like them. Only his essential rootlessness makes him hard to plant bugs on.

PAGES 41-42
"Don't look so good, don't feel so good" conversation courtesy of Mike McNeil when he wasn't feeling so good.

The first movie is of course NIGHT OF THE HUNTER, with Bob Mitchum, Shelley Winters, and Lillian Gish. Mitchum says he got that 'love' and 'hate' tattooed on the knuckles from prison.

The second movie, however, is THE PRODUCERS, Zero Mostel and Gene Wilder. Shpringtime for, uh... you-know-who?

PAGE 43
Quoted passage is from JOURNEY, by William Messner-Loebs.

PAGE 44
This quick-healing thing has many variables, and as many drawbacks as advantages.

PAGE 46
Emma keeps a lot of locks on her door, doesn't she?

PAGE 48
No, Emma isn't Jaeger's mother. It's just a manner of speaking.
St. Podkayne— Martian saint from Heinlein

PAGE 49
Botanical gardens are very common in Anvard, closed off from fresh air as it is; the require expert attention to cultivate, cut off from natural sunlight as they are.

PAGE 50
Brain damage is a tricky thing, even for him.

PAGE 51
Lots of bipeds. Fewer quadrupeds than bipeds in the animal kingdom.

PAGE 52
Our first center-stage construct, a raccoon-faced animal keeper. He has four fingers and a thumb, which is commonly illegal for constructs unless they have a job-related need for the full complement of digits. Those that 'have' can pass for non-constructs, and so are hotly resented by 'have-nots' and many non-constructs. He was originally designed to be an accountant.
Notice the dogtags around his neck; no construct appears in public without these ID cards. Being an unconventional construct, his freedom is even more restricted than usual— he cannot leave the zoo grounds unescorted, not even into the parking lot.

PAGE 55
This guy's outfit and hairdo courtesy of my ex-Mormon pal Jason. The hair's bright blue and/or purple. The car is a Pontiac Mako prototype which was never produced.

PAGE 57
Songs on radio: I WAS BROUGHT TO MY SENSES, Sting; LADY NOBLE, folksong, probably pure Ren-Faire; RESCUE ME, Fontella Bass.
The little character in the window is Smut, mascot of the Comic Book Legal Defense Fund. Created and donated by Neil Gaiman.

PAGE 59
On the sign: Arabic, Miremai, and Laeske under the English. 'Miremai', the traders' language, is spoken more or less by most itinerants in this region. The root word, 'miremne', means 'unclean'.
Anvard is a twenty-four-hour city, dividing the day into twelve double-length hours instead of twenty-four. People live on three different 'shifts', the better to cut down on street traffic. It's as if there are three populations, three cities under one roof.

PAGE 61
This is the Painwright's 'oracle'. It doesn't predict the future except as suits its purposes. It's possible that is not always nefarious. People who can't talk anybody else talk to the oracles in the cultural museums, many of which are far more benevolent.

PAGE 63
That is indeed Jaeger's mother on the panel behind him; no, he didn't see her.

PAGE 65
Emma's speech is partly inspired by Terry Gilliam's 12 MONKEYS. 'Psychologically divergent' was at one time a popular PC euphemism within the mental health community. I mean, the nuthouse.

PAGE 66
And this is Brigham Grosvenor. Ex-husband of Emma, father of Rachel, Lynne, and Marcie; ex-Army officer and Root Of The Problem.

PAGE 67
These are nasty scenarios, 'might-happens', presented by the oracle. Given its nature, it almost never presents a happy outcome. Like a nasty Magic 8-Ball.

PAGE 70
People with hyperactive immune systems are often prone to blinding headaches. Teeny, tiny character portraits. I'm not about to try to list them all.

PAGE 71
Unusual blond Medawar; his hair didn't darken in the usual way. People like him are accepted as variations only after a great deal of scrutiny. Clans are often very scrupulous about what kind and how much variation is permitted in their members.
The patterns on their faces are 'war paint', topically psychoactive mixtures applied to enhance various abilities in the wearer, such as concentration, fine motor control, patience, aggression, peripheral vision. Different substances are identified by different colors, different patterns produce subtle effects.

PAGE 72
The 'First Families': the clans. Each clan has a distinctive look for all its members, not only distinctive dress but a physical look and temperament to which each member conforms. They are the ruling class. people who work for them compose the middle class, and 'everybody else' makes up the poor.
The Brownways are the older, lower levels of the city, which are less clean, less safe, and less well-lit the further down you go. The Brownways are mostly inhabited by 'everybody else'. The territory is subject to rolling power brown-outs.

PAGE 73
Poster on front of desk: Constructs are usually identified by their hands. Any construct which has the bad luck to end up in a precinct house will need legal protection.

Pete's a local organizer. Not quite a mob boss, more like a street boss. Layabouts like Jaeger appear and disappear, do jobs for him or men like him.

PAGE 74

This marks the first appearance and continuing ubiquity of the Finder symbol. Just one of those slippery cultural symbols. Doric, Ionic, and Corinthian columns are just bank architecture to us.

PAGE 76

Jaeger sometimes uses his tattoo as a timer. His body won't let him keep it, it fades away in time. The more stress he's under, the faster it fades. Jaeger lives on autopilot. When his tattoo starts to go, he starts wanting to go too.

This is the first time we see Brigham in the flesh. Brig's looks are based on those of a friend of mine, but Brig is older and more portly. 'How not to be seen', Jaeger style. When he was younger, he was a little naive about his abilities. He thought everybody could simply not be noticed unless they wanted to be.

Out in West Texas, where trees are sparse, hawks like to sit on lampposts. At dusk when the lights are lit, you can't see them. Neither can the rabbits. It's quite something to watch them swooping between parked cars in hot pursuit of jackrabbits, which are often far too big to hide under the cars.

Texas. It's a whole 'nother country.

PAGE 77

Jaeger didn't take these pictures— at least, not with a camera. He heisted 'em from Emma's family albums.

PAGE 78

Both Lynne and Marcie have neuro-cranial jacks set into their skulls. Marcie's is far more complex than Lynne's, and was put in specifically to combat her chronic illness by regulating her body right from the command center Quite a few people in Anvard have these things, as it make accessing information and 'virtual real estate' much easier. Kuai Hua brand vital signs monitor. Kuai Hua means 'mallow blossom', and is symbolic of the power of magic against evil spirits. Chinese traditional medicine is very... orderly and complex.

The device itself is capable of monitoring and manipulating very subtle aspects of a patient's body through the cranial jack. In this case, it's meant to be running a series of simple programs designed to bring Marcie's hyperreactive immune system into equilibrium long enough for her to get well.

Lynne, being too smart and wayward to keep her hands off the thing, is inserting her own program riders.

On dresser: King Henry doll. All that's left of the illustrious history of Henry VIII, once king of England, is this traditional child's toy.

PAGE 79

SGI IRIX, anyone? Nobody knows I'm a Luddite.

PAGE 80

Dad has no use for a photo of his middle child.

PAGES 81-84

I learned something important doing these pages. If you're writing a verbal fight, be EXTRA careful to act the lines out yourself, out loud. If you feel dopey saying any part of it, it's badly written. Brig has a simple bar-code-like tattoo; it's a prison thing. Many of the clans despise permanent marking.

Top of page 84— this is a very simplified way of describing the policy which built Imperial Rome.

PAGE 85

Emma is a rather exclusive landscaper/gardener. She doesn't advertise or solicit, she gets handed gingerly from patron to patron Her calling cards are hard to come by.There are lots of parks and gardens, tucked into corners of the middle and upper levels. On rooftops, on terraces, alongside pedestrian bridges, strung between high-rises. Many people set aside space in their houses for 'garden rooms'. It takes skill and talent and advanced education to create these mini-biospheres with only recycled air and artificial light. Note the Finder pattern around the ornamental fishpool.

PAGE 86

Originally, I was going to run this page in full color, since it's our first brief glance into Emma's interior life. Didn't work out.

PAGE 87

Little Blythe Spirit! Given how disoriented and haphazard Emma's life is, she has to have somebody to order groceries and balance the books, answer the phone and pay bills. That somebody is Blythe, Emma's personal A.I. She buffers Emma from the outside world. With her help, she can get through life and be thought of only as flaky, not actually crazy. The world needs its visionaries. Villian Danceny. 'Danceny' comes from the Callow Youth character in Les Liaisons Dangereuses, by Choderlos De Laclos. 'Villian' is such a common misspelling of 'villain' that I just had to give somebody that name. In feudal days, the word 'villain' meant only 'inhabitant of a village'.

PAGE 88

Blythe's virtual conscience gives her headaches, but she and others like her are given entirely too much responsibility to have no ethical structure. Everybody gets the 'one and zero' joke, right? Goood. DON'T SMOKE IN BED, written by Willard Robinson. Sung by Peggy Lee, one of the sexiest singers of the jazz era (and quite a good actress, at that).

Edith Piaf was a sweet canary-voiced French singer, very popular in the '20s and '30s.

PAGES 89-90

This is a British folk song, but I don't know much else about it. I first heard it in THE WICKER MAN, one of the best bad movies ever made, good trash as only the 70's could deliver.

The little Spring ceremony the Medawar girls are enacting can also be seen in this cheesy flick. It still took place in rural areas of Britain in the early part of this century, but has pretty much died out now. The custom went back all the way to the Roman grain-goddess Ceres. We've lost so many funky customs in this century! Where I'm living the kids don't even trick-or-treat on Halloween anymore.

The purpose of this scene was to show how uniform the Medawars are, and how separate Rachel felt in the few years she was living only with her father's people.

PAGE 91
Lynne planted a bug on one of Jaeger's boots. She knows he only has one pair.

PAGE 93
'In the black' did not then and does not now refer to my bank account.

PAGE 94
More walking tours! Jaeger would say that Medina teaches valuable lessons in the perils of beaten paths. In truth, it's probably just the city-dweller's common hostility towards out-of-towners. Small cameo, bottom right corner: Shanda Bruin from SHANDA THE PANDA.

PAGE 95
Although Jaeger does usually get eight hours' sleep in a full day's time, he rarely gets more than a few hours at a time His tendency to drop off wherever he happens to be can leave casual acquaintances with the impression that he's lazy as hell and sleeps constantly. He hates mattresses; they hurt his back.

In the city of Javecek, commemmorations are left on walls or nearby, wherever a person has died. It's considered grossly disrespectful to tamper with them or paint over them, so the casual walker may find them on the restroom floor at a fancy restaurant, by the sides of the road, on the walls of alleys— but surely all over the walls of hospitals.

PAGES 96-97
Is this a dream, a memory, the future? The content of the vision is made up of voluntary euthanasia, the root meaning of the word 'sacred', and the old idea od eating sin. A sin-eater cleanses the dying of all moral stain, taking them all onto himself, usually by the symbolic act of eating food laid out near or actually on the body of the dying. The Javeceki, with their obsession with disease, take thos one step further. Sin-eating is often seen as an advanced form of scapegoating. The sin-eaters themselves are encouraged to think of it as heroism.

Whiskey Jack again — at least, for the moment.

PAGE 98
Jaeger has to be good and wired to stand up in front of a crowd and call attention to himself. He can draw one to him if he needs to, and no flip out much, but if he were to walk out onto a stage with a crowd already there— oh, he'd bug. He'd dive off the stage and start beating the crap out of whoever he could reach. Stage fright's funny that way.

PAGES 99, 100, 101
Yes, for years I dreamed of giving my VCR the same treatment, and last January I finally did! I got a new VCR and an eight-pound maul for my birthday, and spent a happy half an hour beating the bejesus out of the cussed thing. The packaging on electronic equipment always warns the buyer to be careful, because the stuff's so fragile? They're right. But I still didn't have the nerve to do it until I had a new one.

PAGE 102
Pete, unhealthy gangster, first mentioned on Page 73. He is a Medawar by birth, but a marginal one; full membership in a clan is not only determined by your pedigree. The farther down the power-scale of a clan you go, the more it resembles a street mob. Pete isn't a cop or a soldier, but he's still a Medawar, and that gives him a certain authority in the streets. The very pregnant Medawar woman leaning on her walking stick? SHE'S a mob boss. Not a heavy hitter, mind you; sort of a junior lieutenant.

There is no Welfare or government assistance for the poor in Anvard. The clans do believe in helping the poor, but not necessarily in charity. In other words, they often expect favors, loyalty, that sort of thing, in exchange for their help.

The song is THE OBVIOUS CHILD, Paul Simon.

PAGE 103
Radio DJ is an A.I., like Blythe.

First mention of the Pastwatch Institute, which is largely responsible for the garbled renditions of current consumer products' presence in Anvard.

PAGE 104
Boot Camp flashback for Jaeger. The guy who told me this story is named 'Lance'.

So why doesn't Jaeger try to, ah, adjust himself? Anybody who's ever stood up in front of a drill sergeant can tell you about the rabbit-in-the-headlights paralysis that sets in. Whatever he did, he'd'a ended up doing push-ups.

PAGE 105
Why is Brig watering the plants instead of using the facilities inside the house? Well, going in seems like an imposition on a woman who didn't invite him in.

PAGE 108
'Herod's Evil' is not usually a contagious disease. But in the city of

Javecek, many normally nonvirulent diseases become so. Brigham is a Medawar. His clan dominates both the police force and the territorial army of Anvard. His particular family are traditionally polic.

Brig, having lost status by marrying outside his clan, was shifted into the army. It's the closest these clans have to banishment for their own members. Now that he has no place in either force, his disgrace is complete.

Doing other people's dirty work comes naturally to a sin-eater, whether he likes it or not.

PAGE 109
In the eyes of the clans and society as a whole, Jaeger and Brigham are both 'untouchables'. Brig still doesn't act as if he knows it.

PAGE 110
The men commemmorate the place where Emma Hellena Davis died in the Javeceki way, alien to the people of Anvard. The custom is enjoying a brief fad; most Anvardians view such monuments as being in rather poor taste.

PAGE 111
All members of Llaverac clan look female. This is not a sex-segregated school; you are looking at both boys and girls.

PAGE 114
The move begins! Yes, Jaeger did have something to do with Emma getting her dream house. That's what he got from Pete, for a series of favors. It suits him to keep Emma and her kids mobile.

PAGE 115
Some parts of Anvard are like caverns, others are more like the Mall Of the Twilight Zone, pastel rooms and painted girders and trees in pots for miles and miles. The vistas collect tourists.

PAGE 116
Lotta public TVs in this town. Most of the middle class don't keep TVs in their houses, for several reasons: the TV stations are also the manufacturers of the sets, and market pressures have produced TVs that can't be turned off. Also, each station's set is engineered to receive only that station's programming, so you'd have to have a bank of multiple TVs in order to see the bewildering range of channels in any representative sample.

What most people do when they want to veg out is clod-hop down to the neighborhood theater, which maintains several screens and shows everything you could expect to see on the boob tube. Each separate auditorium is usually dedicated to a specific channel.

The difference between a shop or restaurant in an alley and one inside a building is cleanliness and lighting.

The book being discussed is THE KILLER INSIDE ME, a frighteningly

brilliant book by classic noir author Jim Thompson. In Anvard, the book

was recovered by the Pastwatch Institute. The movie made from it is

composed mostly of cobbled-together footage of real events. Filmmakers see it as the ultimate cinema verite.

In traffic, panel 1— Laeske runner. the big lizards are true nomads and live almost entirely on the streets.

PAGE 117
Rachel's using a common device to tune into the soundtrack of a local TV station, not dissimilar to the one Emma used to 'carry' her A.I., Blythe. Anvardians live almost entirely in artificial light, partly from the dome (which they can't turn off) and the streetlights, which they can. As I've said before, theirs is a truly twenty-four hour civilization. Work, play, and school go in three four-hour shifts (eight hours, to us). This keeps street traffic and overcrowding down to what the inhabitants consider a tolerable level.

A family may get up at what would be to us eight AM, get school and work over by four PM, play and relax until midnight, sleep, and repeat. Or they may get up at four and run the cycle from there, or start from midnight.

Night and day are pretty much what you say they are, but the three time demarcations are pretty rigid for work and school, so people's circadian rhythms, once set, tend to keep them on that single schedule. So, if you're a kid in school, your grade will be divided into three separate classes based on time of day, and you may never meet the kids in the other two sub-classes at all. And so on. The effects of the vast crowd of the hours are all around you.

PAGE 120-124
This is an obsessive daydream. This is running through Brig's head half the time. he's only barely aware of it. It starts up when he feels thwarted or manipulated. It burns him into violent rages sometimes, and he doesn't know what's doing it to him.

The intractability of this fantasy animal is drawn from hounds.

Being a member of a clan, and marrying outside that clan, is romanticized by some people, But the culture shock of doing so is often insurmountable. In Brig's case, he just can't understand emotionally why his wife and kids don't 'act right', although intellectually he knew they wouldn't. The very homogeneity that the clans prize creates a terrible craving in some of their members for 'something different'. Non-clan people are much more accustomed to variations in personality, physiology, and psychology, and handle the croosing of social lines with less distress.

Note Brig's hair: the police usually wear their hair short. The army's far more freewheeling and piratical.

PAGE 124
Marcie's dream-bubble contains a butterfly. This was s'posed to refer to two things: the Greek symbol for the psyche was a butterfly, and also the classic solipsistic story about the Chinese philosopher who woke from a dream of being a butterfly, not knowing which was reality. marcie looks much too babyish here. She's small for her age, but she shouldn't be that small.

'Rensie' was one of Will Eisner's pseudonyms.

PAGE 125
Mature Medawar women wear their hair in elaborate braids. Not all of it is their own. Some of it is the hair of their ancestresses, pinned on as braids or woven into their own hair. This is a

defining custom of Medawar womanhood. After death, their heads are shaven, and their hair partly distributed among their descendants, and partly braided into elaborate knotworks which are not worn but kept in the family shrines. It's a form of ancestor worship.

This is Lady Sethra, well-placed in her clan and boss mare of her family, but not as powerful as she acts.

PAGE 126
Milady's family does know that Brig is out of jail. This is their oblique, resentful way of warning Emma that trouble is rumbling on the horizon. Were Emma not alientated from her own clan, the grapevine would take care of the rest.

PAGE 127
The centaur's face is reminiscent of another of my housemates'. Skoptsy cabs— the Skoptskys were a bizarre Christion cult for whom the rejection of sexuality, evangelism, and the doctrine of 'if thy hand offend thee, cut it off' were a volatile mix. They violated other doctrines by practicing self-castration. All the pink bits had to go, including women's breasts. Some believed in forced conversion, for which they were burned out, banned, and shunned by every other Christian cult. Some few still remain in modern Eastern European countries, bizarrely enough, as cab drivers.

Panel 5. Smud Burger sign on cartop is from the remarkable AKIKO ON THE PLANET SMOO by Mark Crilley.

Bottom tier— not all clan people live in neighborhoods dmoinated by their own clan, but most do. Such neighborhoods are naturally very insular.

PAGE 128
In spite of being the result of a cross-clan marriage, Rachel still has a chance to establish herself in her mother's clan. She fits a lot of the Llaverac criteria, and if she competes successfully in what is like a cross between a beauty pageant and a cat show, she could find herself breaking into a world of privilege otherwise closed to non-clan people.

Of course, she thinks her mother's people are all crazy, and she is not attracted to male Llaveracs in the slightest.

PAGE 130
Emma, like many of her clan, engages in an intensive form of meditation. For some, it's just an excuse for histrionics. They behave like unbalanced actors. For others, it's a way of reeling in the hyperactive imagination and high-strung emotions common to their clan.

Emma's have come to dominate her life. She feels so out of control that she spends more and more time trying to get herself back together by meditating, and consequently is spending too much time in that strange, dreamlike, disorienting state to get herself straight between sessions. I have no idea who wrote the song she's singing. I used to hear it in older Warner Brothers cartoons, so it must have been

a popular song of the thirties. Nobody in Anvard has ever heard it, which is why Blythe is compelled to note it down. Information is currency to an A.I., so she cannot simply record it without her mistress' permission. To her, that would be like stealing the silver.

PAGE 131
These are just random bums from another street crew, not Pete's but a member of Sylvan clan's. They're roustabouts like Jaeger, belonging to no particular clan. Alliances on the street are somewaht fluid, at least for people of no clan.

PAGE 132
The address on the card is a fake address. Jaeger set Brig up with this fake place, filled with thrown-away stuff that belonged to his family, painstakingly arranged to make it look like they really live there. His buddies in the street mobs helped him set it up.

PAGE 134
Brig's old leather jacket has a big patch on the back which shows his chapter affiliation. The military clan into which he was born begins the training of its young people very early. Prior to entry into the army or police, all boys are trained in like fashion, divided into troops called chapters, each roughly equivalent to a company. The chapters vary a lot in demeanor, from prep-school stuffy to good ol' boy to biker club. The Red River is not terribly spit-and-polish.

PAGE 135
This city is home to many animals, some fairly large, who evade captors through the tangled-up alleyways but still sometimes get hit by cars. They're like those birds who fly into warehouse-style groceries and set up housekeeping there: building nests in the rafters, chowing down the fresh produce, dropping what they will on the shoppers' heads, and resisting all attempts to eject them.

Panel 5. In the family portrait, Lynne's face is obscured by a smaller photo of Marcie. Brig arranged it that way while cleaning, but Lynne would have done the same.

Panel 6. this is a free-man license. It looks like a big heavy ring, but it is in fact a neural plug. It fits into a jack at the base of the subject's skull. This is a regulatory device for parolees convicted of violent crime.

PAGE 136
Emma's REAL apartment, which is busily being packed up, is a good few cubic miles and traffic headaches away. Even a crow can't fly a straight line in Anvard.

PAGE 137
This Medawar man is neither a cop nor a soldier, but a priest of a revived god named Huitzilopochtli, of Aztec origin. He was the state god of the Mexica, and like many such was believed to require regular human sacrifice to survive. He has been reinterpreted as the god of the public's lust for gory stories about murder, highway accidents, and other gruesome, violent things.

The priest's war paint is applied to enhance memory, attention span, and visual acuity.

The kid who shot this film was Ruth, who runs the streets with Brig's middle kid Lynne. She and her crew got a lot of money for it.

The white-haired guy with the patterns on his hands is named Eval. He's the only one of the lot who is a member of a clan— Sylvan clan, to be exact.

PAGE 138
The guys all know the address is fake. They helped set it up and furnish it. Eval was there to make sure it looked lived-in.

PAGE 139
All Llaveracs are viewed with some suspicion, since one never knows whether one is dealing with a male or a female until you get her pants off.

PAGE 140
Jaeger's hide is like leather, Rachel's got to scratch him rather hard if she wants him to feel it. She's known since she was a kid that he really likes having his back scratched; she just doesn't know it turns him on.

Jaeger's got the sniffles. For him this means he's been taking it too easy, and his chronic illness is making a comeback. He needs a physical shock to throw it off.

PAGE 142
Eval, as a member of Sylvan clan, has a certain talent for objective magic. He can't do much besides manipulate smoke and mist into figures, but he's quite good at that.

Down at the bottom of the page, Marcie is holding a small wire-globe toy.

PAGE 144
These few impressions, along with intense anxiety, are all Marcie remembers of her family's escape from her father. The smell of hot chrome will bring it back sometimes, and her little wire toy both fascinates her and makes her a little queasy.

'Ne kulturny' is a Russian insult, menaing literally 'uncultured'. Equivalent to 'ya ignorant slob'. If you don't recognize THIS quote, go read your Thoreau, ya ignorant slob!

PAGE 145
The city, almost entirely enclosed by its dome, has troubles with fresh air. The dome does have a few big holes in it, but the city is so built up inside it that these aren't anywhere near enough to provide enough airflow. Air-scrubbers keep the air clean and circulating— when they work. When they break down, out comes the Fog Squad. Medawar police, naturally. Every building, house, and car is supposed to be airtight and equipped with a backup air supply. The guys can't smoke because the truck's air supply isn't very sophisticated— just a couple bottles of oxygen. Jaeger smokes a lot in town because his sense of smell is very acute. Outside cities, he depends on the stuff far less.

The 'ceiling' is not the roof of the dome. We are at the level of the river her, and the dome is far, far overhead. This semi-enclosed cavern is one of many such open spaces.

PAGES 146-149
Here's that physical shock he was needing.

In the center panel of page 147, you can just see the bug Lynne put on the sole of his boot.

Page 149— the little song Emma is singing is from Rogers and Hammerstein's THE KING AND I. It is performed by Lady Chiang, head wife, to explain her devotion to her semi-barbaric husband.

Da-DAHHH! Enter Terry Ellis Lockhart, Emma's father, who is (sadly) just another character I don't have enough time to do anything much with just yet. Terry Ellis is a very rich and powerful member of Llaverac clan. Terry Ellis IS MALE, though she'd slap my head off my neck for saying so. The semi-toxic river water gives Jaeger the last of what he needs to shrug off his decline into sickness. He may lose his hair, his smokes, and his clothes (including the boot with the bug), but he'll be fine. If he didn't do this kind of thing, he'd just get sick and get sicker, never get well until he did something heinous enough to himself to counteract it.

PAGE 150
Terry Ellis and his wife Marion look like they're years and years apart. This is partly custom, and partly vanity. Terry Ellis is in fact the elder by quite a bit, although of course asking about it is another slapping offense. Llaveracs favor at least ten years' difference in age between married people, and in this Terry Ellis and Marion are typical. Marion herself is unusual, in that she has not undergone any kind of rejuvenation program.

So: Jaeger made his way to a fog-addled drop straight down to the river, which is hemmed in by bridges and buildings. He let the river carry him down a way, then climbed out and started climbing back up. He's done this before and he knew he was upstream of the fake apartment, already vacated by Brigham. Buildings are built every which way in Anvard, on top of each other and the lattice framework of the dome. He's got a long way to climb, but this keeps him healthy. Once in the apartment, he snitched Brig's free-man license.

A 'fritillary' is a type of butterfly. 'The Golden Fritillary' is a huge department store in a book by Joan Slonczewski called DAUGHTER OF ELYSIUM.

PORTRAITS